© 2021 Copyright David Lady

Imprint: Independently published,
Ocala Florida, USA

All rights reserved.

This is a work of fiction. Any resemblance
to actual events or persons, living or
dead, is entirely coincidental.

AUTHOR'S NOTE

The Smalls is based upon an idea that I have been kicking around for two decades. I'm calling it horror/suspense, which it is, but it is also a mashup of genres, including the thriller and even transcendental philosophy.

It's hard to pen a completely unique story nowadays. Still, I think we get close with *The Smalls* as it is a horror suspense transcendental philosophical thriller. And it takes place in 1919 and 1920, so we can add *historical* to the mix.

This story is in my *Purgatory Oaths* series. The series can be read in any order; it carries a unique and consistent literary style and theme and revolves around an interesting preternatural concept. I want to write here and explain all kinds of things, but they would give pieces of the universe away, so this will need to be a short note.

This is my sixth book and tenth published work, counting some short stories. I have pushed the boundaries of my comfort zone to give the narrative and characters justice. Well, we can have a long chat after you read *The Smalls* and debate if *justice* is the proper term.

I hope you enjoy reading *The Smalls*; keep a light on!

D. Edward

MINNEAPOLIS, MINNESOTA

JULY 16, 1914

"I don't fully understand how the thingy works." Kathy Gates put her teacup down and looked at Ed skeptically. Charles, her husband, had left the room moments ago, sold on the idea but off to another business meeting, letting Mrs. Gates work out the details. She ran the estate house anyway, so this was just one more thing.

Hello Ed, I love you, do you know that?

The room was hot. Ed was sweating. The damn voice was back. It was going to mess up the biggest sale of his life.

"You said there are two parts to it?" Mrs. Gates wrinkled her brow waiting for Ed to explain.

Ed was momentarily confused; who was talking?

There are three parts, Ed, not two. How many times do I have to tell you? Ed screamed *Shut up, you!* to the voice on the inside, trying to focus his own thoughts.

He recovered with a moment of clarity, as sometimes happened. "Yes, ma'am." He sounded cheery and salesman-like when he said it, even though he was confused about what was going on.

Always tell the client they are right even when you are about to correct them, Ed thought to himself; his voice in his head was different from the *other* voice in his head. He could usually distinguish them.

He continued. "There is an evaporator, compressor, and condenser. We'll put part of the system outside of the house and part of it inside. Then you can simply pick a temperature, and the unit will make the air in the room that temperature!"

Those aren't the parts we talked about, Ed. Tell her about the three parts of her soul. That's good stuff; it's philosophical. These old bags eat that stuff up. Then we can start collecting like I told you.

He had to keep talking. *Don't let it distract you!*

Was that his voice or the other one?

"What it does is it separates the hot air from the cool air. It leaves the hot air outside and pushes the cool air inside."

Ed had to concentrate so much, he was drenched in sweat. He used a handkerchief to wipe his brow, smiling the whole time. He heard someone explaining the hot-air cool-air thing.

Had that been him? *No, Ed, I said it. You*

wondered off. I had to save the day again.

Shut up, you! We need this sale to start the project.

The voice remembered. Ed was right. The voice went quiet.

"You see, Mrs. Gates,"—*I can think again, thank God!*—"everything in the world has three parts. The Chinese call it yin and yang. In America, you call it positive and negative.

"In Russia, where I am from, we would say *'tolkay i tyanay.'* The push and the pull.

"Here, we have the air like it is right now." He put his hands up to suggest air. "See, that's the first thing. Then we have the air we want and the air we don't want. That's two and three.

"In the summer, we don't want the hot air; we want the cool air. In the winter, the other way around." Ed waved his arms this way and that to suggest which air she wanted and which air she didn't.

Mrs. Gates was nodding; it all seemed very scientific, but she was following along just fine.

"So what the air handler does is condition the inside air to include the parts we want and to remove the parts we don't want. It separates air into pieces." *Here comes the big close. It gets them every time.* "If only we could use this on the like of our family members!" *Big smile; let her know it's our little joke together.* "We could keep just the parts of them we like the best!"

Laugh some, get her going.

Mrs. Gates snorted, immediately putting her hand over her nose and mouth. Snorting was so unladylike. Then laughing again, she couldn't help it. The joke rang true; she was sold.

Ed, I like the way you think! Let's start separating now. Start with her!

Shut up, you!

CHICAGO, NASHVILLE, ATLANTA, MIAMI

1914–1919

Ed Leeds sold air conditioners for the Carrier Air Conditioning Company of America for the next five years. The conversations went about the same as the Gates sale. He had three meetings a day, six days a week, and closed sixty-five percent of his pitches.

It wasn't all salesman magic. The Carrier office had a team of people finding leads. Ed only got the appointment once the client had agreed they wanted a unit. Still, Ed had the highest closing percentage of any salesman.

As the joke went, "We don't call him Ed *Leeds* for nothing!"

He received a commission of eighteen dollars and seventy-five cents for each sale and sold over five hundred units a year. He saved every penny, living off the five dollars per week per diem Carrier provided him. After his fifth year, he had earned, in total, almost sixty-thousand dollars in commissions. Early on, he retained a stockbroker and bought Coca-Cola stock with half his money.

Over the years, he worked his way south, following the buildout of electrical power plants. He spent a season in the major cities heading from Minneapolis to Miami City. His last day at Carrier was at the Miami City office on November 14, 1919, a Friday. The official end of Florida's air conditioning sales season. No one knew it, but he was worth over a million dollars that day, between saved money and the valuation on his stock portfolio.

Prohibition would start in January 1920, in about a month and a half. Ed was excited about it. He didn't drink alcohol, so he wouldn't miss it in its absence, but his Coca-Cola stock should shoot through the roof in two or three months. It would be one of only a few legal means of getting high. The delicious sugar-soaked cocaine-laden drink that tasted best chilled.

"Coca-Cola, it has to be good to get where it is! Seven million a DAY!"

But Ed wasn't happy; he was terrified. He quickly scrambled away from his office, saying his goodbyes, driving his Ford Model-T out of Miami City as fast as he could.

He had until midnight. That was the deal.

He also knew the voice was a liar and a cheat. It didn't honor agreements, so the fact it seemed to have observed this promise, over so long a time, was even more disconcerting.

Ed had worked hard, but he knew this was just the beginning. He had to stop the voice before it acted on its plan. He had to find out whose voice it really was and how they were able to project it into his head.

The days were getting shorter in South Florida this time of year. It was dark at six o'clock in the evening as he drove the dirt back roads, finally reaching Florida City around eight o'clock. He had to be careful; the closest place to get gas for the car was an hour back towards Miami City.

The night was inky black, the temperature was humid but cool, a pleasant seventy degrees.

With nights delights, sales go to jails. He mused that if people were comfortable sleeping, *they don't buy air conditioners.* His work-focused brain was not yet ready to transition to retirement.

The Model-T rumbled into the small center of the small town that was Florida City, a large dirt street with a row of buildings on only one side. A flophouse, a hardware store, a few small markets, the Homestead County building, and the Palm Street Tavern were all in the row.

Ed looked around. There should be more people. He came to Florida City on weekends and generally whenever he could. The location aligned harmonically and magnetically. It was the perfect place for his efforts to stop the voice.

Sometimes he slept in his car. Rarely would he pay the twenty-five cents to get a bed at the flophouse. The tavern had rooms upstairs also, nice ones. But Ed was too cheap to pay the dollar-a-night rate—he had spent the last five years sleeping in his car and looking washed and pressed the next day.

Why just throw money away now? Acquiring the stuff is too much work to waste it.

He turned the car off and listened to the quiet, opening the door as the engine's noise faded away after a few clanks and bonks.

It's so dark. There should be some lights, especially in the tavern. Friday night is their big night. Why aren't the streetlamps lit?

Something caught his eye as it moved across the street. Ed couldn't make out if it was a person or something else. A black shadow was running low and around to the back of the row, down a way.

Why is it so dark out?

He looked up to the sky. No moon and high clouds.

Whispering came from the direction of the tavern. A burst of a loud whisper erupted, then nothing. The sound was scolding. The hair on the back of his neck stood up; the whispering had been so purposeful.

There was another sound across the street;

another black figure moved low then was gone.

Fear grew inside Ed. He wasn't a big man —small, actually. Just over five feet tall and a hundred pounds after a big meal.

He slowly walked across the street, staring into the darkness. If something were over there, he should be able to find it. Whether he wanted to or not was another question. He had no idea what it could be. As he reached the edge of the wide dirt road, he stopped. There were low palmetto bushes for fifty feet on either side, then farther away cypress trees and a low area often muddy with a few inches of water year-round.

Someone was staring at him. The hair on the back of his neck was still standing up; he had that sense of being observed. He could hear the voice starting to stir, deep down, getting restless in waiting for the agreed time. He heard the whispering again, very loud, from behind him.

His name floated in on the wind, then some commotion.

He realized he was frozen and sweating a cold sweat in the pleasant night air. His hands were clenched into fists, not that he could use them to defend himself very well. Finally digging deep and mustering the resolve to move, he turned around, immediately bumping into someone who had approached him silently from behind.

"No, let me go!" Ed screamed, assuming it was

the voice manifested, waving his arms. He felt his heart flutter as he pushed away as hard as he could.

"Ed!" someone yelled. It wasn't the voice. The voice sounded mean, talking with a low rumbling evil that always suggested nefarious intentions. This voice now was high and pleasant.

The person stood about his height. They had been soft when he bumped into them, and they smelled like strawberries.

"Coral?" Ed said, trying to shake the fear away, which wasn't working.

"Ed!" she said again in a smooth and comforting way. "Ed, I'm sorry. I didn't mean to startle you! I saw you walk across the street and came over to say hi."

He knew it was her, but the night was so black he had difficulty seeing her clearly. "I saw two shapes moving over here. Why are the lights out?" He realized she might know.

Coral put her hand on Ed's shoulder. She had been making friendly overtures to Ed for a year; he had been, so far, too dense to pick up on them. "Sorry, Ed, those were the Jones boys. They are meeting their mom inside the tavern and ran from their house the back way."

Why would kids stoop low and run through the darkness hunched over?

He pushed the thoughts away. If Coral said

that's what the shadows were, that's what they were. She still had her hand on his shoulder and was standing very close to him, causing him to continue to sweat. But a different kind of sweat, the fear in the air was changing to something else. Was she moving closer to him?

Suddenly a bloodcurdling wail rang out; it sounded like a small child screeching in terror. It was so loud and yet far away. Ed unconsciously pulled his way into an embrace with Coral, seeking shelter, clutching at her in fear without realizing it, really almost trying to run through her. She was also startled, both of them using the closeness of the other as reassurance.

The screech came again, a sound of terror and agony, followed by a second howl of panic from a slightly different voice.

Coral relaxed but did not push Ed away. "It's bunnies," she said, starting to laugh, leaning into him.

Ed was still terrified and in shock. He pushed her away, stepping out of the impromptu embrace, not happy with her casual dismissal. "Bunnies? What are you talking about?"

The screams came again. It sounded like hell on Earth. Coral continued to giggle.

Ed was mortified and confused, his small frame shaking more violently.

"Sounds like a python has found a rabbit hole. I shouldn't be laughing. What happens is when the snake gets ahold of the rabbit from the back, the rabbit screams and screams as it is being eaten alive. Sounds like two pythons are cleaning up a group of them. It's a lot simpler when they get the rabbit head first, then it suffocates and doesn't suffer so much."

Ed's fear was fading, replaced by confusion and revulsion. "That's horrible! Why would you laugh about it?" He was truly upset about the callousness she had shown.

Coral giggled again. "I'm sorry, I wasn't laughing at the rabbits. I agree that would be crazy insensitive. I was laughing at you." She saw him make a sour face. "NO, in a good way! You were so cute and so worried! It's just one of the noises you get used to hearing living out here on the edge of the Everglades."

Ed looked down; somehow, Coral had managed to be holding his two hands. The situation was getting romantic, the scare flooding both him and her with adrenaline. Coral was so young; he was so old. But more than that, he could never let the voice know about her, about how he thought about her late at night.

The voice would ruin everything, maybe worse.

He let go of her hands and tried to pull himself together. She made a sad face when he let go, her bottom lip out in a pout.

At least the sickening screaming has stopped, Ed thought.

"Why are all the lights out?" he asked again after a few moments of them both standing together in silence.

Coral snapped to like she had been deep in thought. "Oh, the lights!" she called out with glee in her mellow voice, a stark contrast to how Ed felt at the moment. "Come on, that's what I wanted to show you!" She grabbed his hand and pulled him along, heading back to the tavern where she worked, beaming with pride.

She headed straight for the tavern door, pushing it in and confidently entering the dark building. Suddenly Ed's senses were assaulted again, his nerves already frazzled. The inside of the tavern flashed from pure darkness to bright yellow light in an instant. There were a dozen people in the main room who all started yelling "Surprise!" in unison, providing even more tension to the jarring moment.

Ed's heart skipped a beat. He almost fainted, but another wave of adrenaline shot through him, keeping him upright. Then he realized it was a retirement party for him. It was easy to figure out once his eyes adjusted. There was a big hand-painted sign on the back wall that said:

Happy retirement party, Ed!

Ed looked around. He recognized everyone and knew a few of the patrons very well. The room smelled like fresh bread and cake. This meant they had gone all out and that Sally Jones, the owner of the small sundries store a few buildings down, had made Ed a retirement cake. Sally was the best baker that Ed had ever known. He had eaten nearly everywhere, but she had some magic combination of ingredients that somehow were just wonderfully good. Her storefront was one of the main reasons Florida City was on the map; people traveled from a hundred miles away for one of her custom delicacies.

Then a second thought hit him. The lights weren't oil lamps.

"What are the lights? Are they electric?" he said, suddenly distracted.

The mood in the room stayed jovial, the anticipation of the secret they all wanted to share dancing front and center. Everyone was so happy.

A big fat man in a white suit stood up from the bar. "Ed, I always tell everyone you are a quick study!"

Gary Laundry was the town mayor, elected a year ago by a vote of all eighteen eligible male town residents, running unopposed. He would be up for reelection in another three years, the next time needing to seek both male and female votes as the women's suffrage amendment was in the process of state ratification. Given the population growth, he would need to persuade almost fifty people next time, not just eighteen.

He knew the trick to it was to run unopposed; that strategy made politics easy.

Mayor Laundry waved his arm this way and that, indicating several electric lamps on either side of the room. "They just completed the first power run from Turkey Point!" Laundry looked very proud. "It took some doing to get Florida City wired in, but I did it! Your local government at work for you, our prized and cherished citizenry!" He flowed into what must have been part of a political speech he had given recently.

Everyone was excited to see Ed's reaction. It wasn't just that they liked Ed and wanted to impress him. He had announced six months ago that, upon his retirement—and provided Florida City had electrical power—he would purchase a significant amount of land. This represented a lot of money for the new little city. The land in question was currently unincorporated but owned by the newly incorporated town.

Coral was glowing also, genuinely seeming excited and happy that Ed might be retiring close by. "Ed, look outside!" she nearly squealed.

Ed turned around and could see out the still-open tavern door that there was now lamplight meekly peeking in from several places in the front of the buildings. He turned and walked back out to get a better look. There were six lamp posts, each with a yellow bulb giving off light. The inky-black night was fighting hard, but in the small, protected row of buildings along the wide dirt street, modern civilization was beating it, if only just.

Ed was impressed. His fear and concerns from a little while ago were fading. He turned to head back in to enjoy the celebration and spend time with his potential new neighbors. He still had to work out the details for the land, but everything seemed to be falling into place. There were still a couple hours before midnight. Enough time to enjoy being himself before things went back to how they had been in Minneapolis a lifetime ago.

Coral slid her arm into his as she closed the tavern door; they walked in together a second time. As they returned, Pastor Rick Weller started to sing a joyous hymn.

After some song and merriment, Sally brought out a sweet-smelling red and blue cake. It was meticulously made, the surface shiny and flawless. It was a big cake, two feet long and near a foot high. On the top, she had made the figure of Ed, proudly presenting a giant gray box, presumably an air conditioner unit.

When Ed saw it, he could not help himself. He smiled and clapped, feeling true joy and happiness for one of the first times in his life.

A big gruff-looking man behind the bar made a toast. "Ed, we are glad to welcome you to our little community. We have worked hard to make this a place people want to move to, and we hope that you are the first of many to discover our little slice of paradise. As people here already know, I served with Teddy Roosevelt and the Rough Riders. I can speak firsthand to the quality of a person, and Ed, I judge you as top shelf!"

"Speech! Speech!" The chant grew in the room.

Coral urged him forward, walking him to the center of the room, then walking away, leaving him there.

Ed looked around. "Thank you, Mrs. Sally, for the delicious cake. And thank you, everyone, for this gathering. It means more than you might know."

There was laughter and clapping.

"I'm excited to move here and to become your neighbor. I think Florida City has nothing but potential." Ed raised his cake plate as a pseudo toast and took a bite, suggesting his speech was over.

"Boo!" Coral yelled in a fun-spirited way. "Tell us why you needed the electricity!"

The rest of the small crowd seconded the request: "Hear, hear!" and "Yes, tell us!" as well as some just clapping.

"Okay, okay." Ed smiled, growing more uncomfortable now. He couldn't tell them that he needed to build a giant electromagnetic machine to search for and find a person projecting a voice into his head. He couldn't mention that he had been studying ancient engineering principles for the past five years when not selling air conditioner units. That those principles hinted at a relationship between magnetism and gravity that he needed to explore to save his sanity.

Think, Ed!

"I am going to build a giant cathedral!"

The room remained quiet.

Ed smiled.

As everyone just looked at each other and looked back to Ed, Pastor Rick spoke up.

"We have a cathedral here already, son. The Lord's house, my church."

You should have used a different word. Try castle.

"Of course, Pastor, I didn't mean to imply this was a religious endeavor. I should have said a castle, not a cathedral. I plan on building a giant castle out of coral. A coral castle, right here on the edges of the Everglades!"

"Why?" Coral spoke up. Unlike everyone else in the room who looked confused or disappointed, she looked interested.

Ed smiled at her. "That, my pretty barkeep, is a good question!"

He said it jovially enough that everyone laughed. The mild tension left the room. His speech was blessedly over.

Coral came over to Ed as everyone went back to their conversations. "Ed, that's really interesting. A giant castle out here. How fun!"

"This is the perfect place; there are principles at work here. Between being at exact sea level, the flowing tides of the water right below the ground, and some other things."

"Well, don't mind all of them. I think it is a wonderful project!" She leaned in and kissed him on the cheek.

He blushed a deep red.

As the evening progressed, Ed could occasionally still hear the rabbits outside from time to time, screaming bloody murder as they were slowly eaten alive by giant snakes.

CRYSTAL RIVER, FLORIDA

NOVEMBER 15, 1919, 4 A.M.

Isaac Stone sat sloppy drunk on the bar stool in the Fox & Hound pub. The pub was on the corner of Main Street and Second Avenue in the tiny downtown of Crystal River.

He had so far avoided sleep since this past Tuesday, but he knew the cycle and knew there would be no more avoiding it. While he might know about sleep, he didn't know how many highballs he had drunk in the past six hours.

No one might have known. It might not even be knowable. One of many great local mysteries.

Whiskey and Coca-Cola highballs were potent: two shots of eighty-proof whiskey alcohol, cane sugar, and just enough cocaine to blend the night together.

Stone wanted another one. Just one more.

The bartender wanted something too. He

wanted to go home.

The bartender's problem was that Stone was the Citrus County Sheriff. He was the guy you called to get rid of drunks that didn't go home at 4 a.m. when you needed to close. Yes, he could also call the city police, one guy named Jim Johnson. But picking sides like that would be bad for business. Johnson was a one-man show; Stone had eight deputies and good county funding.

A couple hours ago, when Stone was still kind of coherent, they had *the* conversation. They had it most nights about that time. Stone assured him that the Fox & Hound was lucky. Stone would be right here if anyone needed to call the county sheriff to deal with any drunks. Personal service; what could be better?

Stone continued to tap his glass, indicating he wanted another round. "William," he said to the bartender. "William, let's set up another one, please." His words sliding into one another like ice cubes melting on a table.

William walked over to stand in front of Stone. He knew how to talk to him. He also knew that sometimes it worked, sometimes it didn't. "Sherriff, it's 4 a.m., closing time. I believe you have to be at work in a few hours."

Stone lifted his eyes from his empty glass to look at William directly, who was a suspiciously fuzzy blur. "William, you forget yourself, my good man. Today is Saturday. It is my day off. I know this because yesterday was Friday. I work on Fridays but not on Saturdays. Therefore, I am not working since it is Saturday, and I do not have to be at work in a few hours as aforementioned. Thus and hitherto, clearing up this mess and *paving the way,* as the kids say, to my extended patronage."

Stone tapped his glass again, a proud look of victory passing over his face. He felt proud to have worked in modern slang as well. The new roads were paved, the workers literally "paving the way" now wherever you wanted to go.

William cursed Saturday in his head, but not out loud, blowing air out instead and settling in while he poured the whiskey and Coca-Cola into Stone's glass, over the existing half-melted ice.

Jack Abbott, Stone's friend of many years, leaned over to whisper from the stool next to him. Stone leaned over to hear him, then laughed and slapped the bar, looking back to William.

"William, my good ma—uh, friend—Mr. Jack Abbott would like another round as well, please. Thank you."

William moaned internally. *Not this again,* he thought.

Gathering his internal resolve, William said, "Yes, Judge." He used the sheriff's nickname to keep things civil. "However, if you remember, and this was at your own request, Mr. Abbott is not to be served here anymore."

Stone vaguely remembered something about this, but it wasn't what he wanted now. "William, do I look like I was born yesterday?"

William knew this one also. "You look like you're about thirty-five, Sheriff." Now he will say, *Mighty kind, William. I stopped aging at thirty-six; it is true. But that was fifty-five years ago.* William never understood why Stone thought this was a joke or what was funny about it.

"Mighty kind, William. I stopped aging at thirty-six; it is true. But that was fifty-five years ago." Stone snickered to himself, then leaned over and said something in a low whisper, nodding after a bit. "Mr. Abbott would like his drink now, please." He nodded to Abbott and winked.

Abbott returned the gaze, not looking confident about the situation.

"I'm sorry, Sheriff. Mr. Abbott is not to be served here. You said you would come back and shoot me if I ever served him."

"That is outrageous, sir! An abuse of justice and author-roar-we...authority!" Stone finished just as he finally passed out, his head slumping down onto the bar.

William cleaned up the bar, wiping it down. He lifted Stone's head to wipe under it, then, mostly careful, letting Stone's head fall back onto the cold wood surface. Once everything was cleaned up, he went and put his arms through Stone's, up under and around his shoulder to lift him from behind. Stone was heavy, mostly muscle but not all of it. William had to do all this himself, of course, because no one else was there to help. He dragged Stone this way into a small room in the back and, again mostly careful (but not *completely* careful), put Stone on a cot in the little room where he could sleep it off.

As he started to close the door, William turned and looked; the heavy curtain was drawn over the high window. He walked over and opened the curtain. The morning sun would now shine in at around 7 a.m., waking Stone. If everything worked out, Stone would be gone and too hungover to come back tonight when William reopened at 8 p.m.

As Stone laid there unconscious (sleeping would in no way be the correct term), he had a dream. In the dream, Jack Abbott and Maggie Summers were trying to tell him something. Then the dream shifted back to when he died near fifty-five years ago, in the Civil War prisoner camp.

THE REALLY NICE ROOM

NOVEMBER 15, 1919, 7 A.M.

Ed woke up feeling terrific. Everything had gone perfectly. The party was fun, more fun than he had had in a while. The voice didn't return to spoil anything. Bahama Bill Burton, the owner of the Palm Street Tavern and the big scary man who had toasted Ed last night from behind the bar, had given Ed a free room—the nicest one—as part of the town's celebration of his retirement. The bed was soft; the sheets were clean. Even better, the room had indoor plumbing.

Indoor plumbing was not a new invention; many buildings and houses had it and had now for a decade or two. But not all the places Ed stayed did, and if they did, certainly not private facilities. Not with a sink and a shower and hot water to boot.

As he sat up in bed, he could see the sun rising in the east over the Everglades out the window. The pane of the window was open, letting in the cool pleasant overnight breeze.

I'll have to sell against the weather today, he thought to himself.

Then he realized that today was the first day of his retirement. He wouldn't have to sell against anything. Instead, he was the customer, starting the process to acquire the ten acres he needed after the weekend. The townspeople had held up their end—electricity by the time he retired. He could now hold up his end.

He also had to get the work done on the car. He would do that work himself, but it was a big job, maybe three or fours days total if he worked all day. And he needed equipment, blowtorches, and some pulley/winch combo to help get the pieces of the car apart in the back.

You have the car, the parts you don't want, and the parts you do. The trinity of three. Yin and Yang in a Model-T.

Ed froze.

Was that the voice or just my own thoughts?

He waited.

No snarky quip. No moralizing justification to start cutting people up.

He relaxed. It had been his inner voice, just his own thoughts.

Good! It's going to be a great day!

It is!

Ed became icy cold all of a sudden. *Damnit. Hello, voice.*

Hello, Ed. I love you, do you know that? Don't worry, though. I'm not back yet. You're not ready for me. You are still thinking like a salesman. You need more time. You're not retired yet.

Voice, I am a salesman. I will never be ready for you.

Silly! I do have a message for you, though. You need to go to Crystal River. I have something there I made for you that you need to understand. I made it a long time ago, just for you, to show you. I am there now, too, waiting. We can finally meet in person!

Ed felt sick; he didn't want to go to Crystal River. It was two days away, or more, on the other side of the state. But he did want to meet the person projecting the voice. That was important in his quest to get it to stop talking to him.

Ed, go before you do the work on the car, yes? I know this will push back the paperwork for the land, but that's okay. Go today and sleep in your car on the way, like you used to. If you do as I say now, you will have two more weeks of freedom from me.

The voice was gone. He didn't know how he knew, just that he knew. He wasn't happy anymore. He felt terrible now, not good like a few moments ago when he woke up.

Wait, how did the voice know about the car?

The room went from cool to cold to hot. Warmer now than the outside breeze.

Damn. I was looking forward to enjoying a hot shower in the cool air. Now it's just hot like always.

He got up and showered anyway, shaving after with scalding hot water in the sink. Pure luxury.

Once dried off, he put on his salesman clothes. He had planned on his overalls and work shirt, but if he was postponing the car work, driving across the state, he might as well wear his pressed white shirt and gray suit and black tie.

People always responded well to it.

It was seven-thirty in the morning when he came down the stairs into the tavern proper. The place had been cleaned up and looked like it always did. Something smelled good: bacon and eggs and something else.

Bahama Bill sat at one of the tables with Coral. Father and daughter having breakfast together, very much the look of a family. Of course, Coral wasn't his daughter by relations; he had more or less adopted her ten years ago because she had nowhere else to go.

A place at the table had been set for Ed, and he seemed to be walking down exactly when the meal was ready. When Coral saw him, her face lit up.

She made a motion to the open seat. Bahama Bill waved a welcoming wave also, suggesting Ed join them.

He usually wouldn't have. Despite all the interest and attention he was getting, Ed was not a social person. The energy he used during the days to sell air conditioners cost him. He needed every night, and his one day off each week, to replenish the energy being around other people took from him. He also enjoyed his own company more than that of others.

But today, this morning, it was the perfect setup for breakfast with new friends. He was still in the afterglow of the party, he was hungry, he had a long day ahead, and there was nowhere else that he knew of to get a good breakfast in the area.

Coral beamed at him as he sat down. "Ed, you look so professional! But you should relax! You don't have to dress just to visit me."

Did she just wink?

Ed looked down uncomfortably, then glanced at Bahama Bill. If Coral had been his real daughter, Ed doubted he would be so comfortable with her flirting with him so openly.

"Thank you." He didn't know what else to say to the comment.

Coral held her smile, but her eyes changed underneath it. She made a quick glance to Bahama

Bill, trying to keep the smile, quickly looking back at Ed.

Bill cleared his throat, speaking happily even though there was a hollowness to it. "Ed, I thought you were retired and were going to start taking it easy? Why don't we go hunting today, you and me?" He glanced back to indicate a hunting rifle behind the bar.

Ed looked at Bill. "I have some work to do, then I have a matter over near Tampa I have to attend to. So I'll be back in maybe a little under a week."

These are friendly people. This whole town has been charming to me. I wonder why?

Out loud, he continued, "Bahama Bill, I appreciate your offer. It is nice to be back around people that understand family. You all here in Florida City are much more like the people I knew growing up within Russia than a lot of what I saw in all the big cities over the past several years."

Bahama Bill smiled a big friendly smile. "Come on, Ed, we're just regular folks! You pushed Laundry to get the electrical company to run power out here. If it weren't for your encouragement, we wouldn't have power for another five years. And, they wired it to my tavern! I can host movie nights now and raise the cost of the rooms."

Coral leaned in Ed's direction and took his hand, looking into his eyes. "Ed, sometimes things just work out. It is all about surrounding yourself with the right people." She was getting that cat-with-a-mouse look again. "We have another surprise for you! Tell him, Bill!"

Bahama Bill jumped right in. Coral and Bahama Bill seemed to Ed to have such a connected relationship, almost finishing each other's sentences like they had practiced delivering persuasive speeches together.

"We all made Laundry agree to get up early and open the county office for you on the weekend, so you could put your petition in for the land today! He is over there now. You can go right there when you finish breakfast. You don't have to wait until 10 a.m. Monday when the office would normally open!"

That was helpful. Ed realized it would help get him on the road for the trip to Crystal River. He looked over at Bahama Bill and then at Coral. She had somehow managed to get his hands again and was holding them, her big blue eyes looking at him with something he couldn't place.

Is that love and admiration?

Coral wasn't the prettiest girl, she wasn't the slimmest, and her hair wasn't always combed. But Ed had to admit she had a charm. She was smart and quick, and sure seemed to fancy him when he was around.

Could my life really work out such that I escaped

the civil war in Russia, came to America with nothing, became a millionaire in five years, turned fifty, and married a pretty American girl less than half my age? While getting rid of the voice?

Put it out of your head, Ed. Maybe—MAYBE—after you discover who the voice is and stop its plan. MAYBE then, but not before. Not now, that's for sure.

He pulled his hands away from hers. She made the same sad face she had made last night, pushing her lower lip out in a pout. He noticed she had perfect teeth.

That's a weird thing to notice, Ed.

He went back to his breakfast and quickly finished, uncomfortable now in the room. He thanked Bahama Bill profusely after he cleared the plate, then headed out and over to the county office building. He could feel Coral's stare, desperately trying to make eye contact with him. He was careful not to meet her gaze.

The outside morning was beautiful. You sometimes get these mornings in South Florida as the seasons change from fall to winter. Cool air, the humidity breaking overnight, making everything feel crisp and new. The ground and other surroundings were still hot to their core, so a slight mist formed in the air as the sun came up. The cool overnight air worked with the dew to put on a show.

Ed walked past his parked car and into the

county office building. A bell rang when he opened the door. The outside of the building was whitewashed, and it had a nice professional sign. The inside smelled like cedarwood, which hit Ed when he stepped in. The main area was clean and organized. Stairs were leading up to a second level, and a hallway leading to other offices had all been painted white and green. It was a big building, but Ed had never seen anyone working in it when he visited. Probably because he mostly came on weekends and off-hours.

Mayor Gary Laundry sat at a big desk. A well-kempt small older woman sat at a smaller desk near the door. It had been explained to Ed that while Laundry was mayor of Florida City, he also acted as the chief administrator for Homestead County. It was said that Homestead bordered Dade County and primarily covered the Everglades. The Everglades did not have a very high population density, so it was easier to do it this way. Ed didn't know much about American government bureaucracy or hierarchy, so it all sounded reasonable to him.

The old woman started to challenge Ed, but Laundry called out, "Mildred, let him pass, please. That's Ed Leeds! He is the one I have been telling you about." Laundry stood up and walked over, shaking Ed's hand vigorously as he moved him through the room and to his desk near the back.

"How are you feeling today, Ed? Did you sleep

well?" Laundry asked, sitting Ed down in the chair on the other side of his desk.

"Yes, thank you. The weather was very comfortable for sleeping, and the room was exceptional. I slept better than I have in a good while."

Laundry smiled a big smile at him. Everyone here seemed to smile a lot and be pretty happy, Ed noted.

Laundry got right to business. "Ed, I have prepared the paperwork to get started. Since this is county land you are purchasing, we have to follow a few state laws; I can't just give it to you."

Ed nodded; this had all been discussed.

"So the first thing we need to do is file an 'intent to sell' notice. I'll do all that. It means I have to put a listing in the local and state paper. Then we have to have a public meeting. Then have a bid session, so the price is determined by the market.

"I don't think anything will come from any of it, but that's what we have to do. I am going to set the value at eighteen hundred dollars, just like we talked about also. One-hundred-eighty per acre.

"Does that all sound good?"

Laundry watched Ed intently.

So this is how it feels to be on the other side of an air conditioner pitch, Ed thought to himself.

He nodded in reply to the question.

There were only two pieces of land in the whole world aligned harmonically and magnetically for what Ed needed to do. One was here just south of Florida City. The other was east and north in Miami City proper. Ed knew he needed the privacy of the Everglades to get the work done, so this ten-acre was his only real choice.

"Terrific!" Laundry said and smiled, putting a pen in Ed's hand and pushing several sheets of paper over to him. "The top page is your inquiry into the land. The next page is a request to purchase. We need those two to get started. The last page is a credit inquiry; we don't need it now, but we'll need it before the auction if you want to start working on it. You will need to provide your bank information and have a bank representative endorse the back"—Laundry leaned forward and turned the sheet over so Ed could see—"here and here. The bottom sheet is for you. It is the land prospectus, its legal address, that type of thing."

Ed signed the top two forms and handed them back.

Laundry took them and looked at the third form in front of Ed. He stared at it for a long moment, then seemed to force himself to look away.

Laundry put the papers in a nice leather binder. "I'll contact the papers today. I know we can get the information in the local paper by Monday. I know the fella that runs the Gulf Star. The *Miami Herald* qualifies for the state paper. I'll see what I can do. And their office is in downtown Miami City, where I am going right now. I can probably have it run Tuesday or Wednesday. It only has to run for one day to meet the requirement."

Laundry seemed happy. Really, really happy.

TAMIAMI TRAIL

NOVEMBER 15, 1919, 10 A.M.

Highway 41 was a brand-new road. Some parts of it weren't finished yet, but most of the route from Tampa to Miami City was passable. The road was named for its ambition: Tampa to Miami, Tampa-Miami, Tamiami.

The posted speed limit was twelve miles an hour. Ed's Model-T could do up to forty miles per hour, but that was crazy fast. He did allow himself to hit twenty from time to time when no other cars were around and when he was in the middle of nowhere.

They had been draining the Everglades for the past couple of years. There was so much land to be recovered. The Miccosukee Indians lived all around the area. They worked a lot of the sugar cane fields, along with the negroes and the poorer crackers (the working white poor).

The fields were in full harvest now. The horizon heading away from the Miami City area was full of black billowing smoke plumes reaching high into the bright blue sky. Each fire was separated by five or ten miles. The farmers burned the fields before they sent the workers in to harvest the crop. They called it a controlled burn. It made getting to the valuable part of the sugar cane plant much more manageable.

The industry was fascinating. The cane, once harvested, was moved to a refinement facility in northern Miami City, where it was broken down into its base sugar. The facility smelled terrible but ran day and night this time of year. Once refined (to a degree), the sugar was put on rail cars and moved up the East Coast on Henry Flagler's FEC Railway. FEC just stood for Florida East Coast. Once in Jacksonville, it was moved to another railway, ultimately ending up at the Coca-Cola factory in Atlanta, Georgia.

Ed knew all this because he researched the entire process before he bought his Coca-Cola stock. It all sounded good, but he wasn't going to invest thousands of dollars into a company whose supply chain he did not understand.

To him, driving on Highway 41, seeing all the cane field fires, he knew it was money in the bank.

Come on, prohibition! he thought to himself with a smile. He felt pretty good and started to enjoy the feeling of freedom on the open road.

Hello, Ed. I love you, do you know that?

He was taken by surprise; the car swerved. He quickly got it back under control.

"Why do you always say that?" Ed felt feisty. He also decided to talk out loud since they were alone. This would make it easier for him to know which voice was his and which belonged to the voice in his head.

Don't worry, I'm not back. I told you I wouldn't be for a while yet. But I want to talk to you. We're friends now, and I just want to explain something to you while we have time. We have several hours now driving. This is as good a time as any.

"So answer the question then." Ed wasn't going to put up with the typical ambiguity today.

Ed, when I talk to you, I always tell you the truth. I tell you I love you because it is the first thing I think about every time we get the chance to talk.

"Who are you?"

Oh, Ed, I have been waiting a thousand years for someone to ask me that. Can you believe it? So long, and no one has ever cared enough to ask me who I am.

"So tell me then, so I know your name when we meet."

I'm so happy, Ed. You have made me so happy. I want to tell you. I will. We're friends, right? My name is IX-Chel.

It sounded in Ed's head like Zee-Shell, with the CH strongly emphasized. The name didn't mean anything to Ed, but it did sound weird. The dialect didn't register as any of the languages he knew. It wasn't English, Spanish, or Russian. It sounded old; the inflection on the second word sounded violent.

No, Ed, the opposite. I am the goddess of love and rebirth! I am the opposite of war and strife. I provide balance and insight.

Something struck Ed as alarming in those words. "You consider yourself a goddess? That's blasphemy!"

I don't know that word, Ed. What do you mean?

"There is only one God and his savior Jesus Christ!"

Ed, we both know you are not religious. Not that kind of religion, anyway. You attend church, but you don't believe it. You know I already know that. That's one of the reasons I picked you. That's one of the reasons we can talk; it's why we can be friends. The slightest edge slipped into the voice.

"You don't know what I believe any more than I know what you believe. But I'm interested. Tell me how you are a goddess."

Ed, you are doing well! You are asking all the right questions. I am so proud of you. I will tell you. You drive; I'll explain how things really are. It will help us in the work ahead so you can understand.

"I'm all ears."

The voice began the story:

There is so much to explain. Let me start by explaining what a god is; there is a common misconception. I hear from so many that it is thought that gods created mankind. That we made people.

Nothing could be farther from the truth! You and I, now, are in the fifth age of mankind. There have been four great worldwide civilizations before now. Each destroyed, the last one in fire and strife.

Each new age brings about new gods. See, the epoch ends when there are no more gods left to be worshipped. We hold the fabric of humanity together. Keep your thoughts organized so that civilization can exist.

But what is a god? That's one of your questions.

A god is a belief manifested. But not just any kind of belief, a special kind. One that extends out of a person and into the universe around us. A god cannot exist without believers. The more people that believe, the more powerful the god is.

Ed, you should have seen me a thousand years ago. I had millions of believers. I was so powerful and so beautiful. If a mortal gazed directly at me, they often went mad, sometimes scratching their eyes out. Once they saw me, true beauty, in my tangible form, they could not bear to look at anything else. It was glorious!

It was such a fantastic time. My whole existence was nothing but pleasure and harmony. My days and nights were filled with entertainment, and no whim went unfulfilled.

At some point, I had so many believers that I transcended power. I could change the world with just my thoughts. I could grant rewards or inflict punishment by just thinking about what I wanted to happen and who I wanted it to happen to. I was wrath and mercy incarnate!

But over time, I lost believers. Not because of me! No! I was the perfect deity. But many of my believers died away in the great plagues. After that, I was replaced by new people with new beliefs in different gods. It was a slow process for me, losing a few believers each day. It was painful and sad.

A few years ago, after a millennium, I was almost gone, my last believers running a side street antique store. Their only belief in me was in the money my trinkets brought in with the tourists.

Can you believe that, Ed? Me, reduced to a sideshow figurine in a tiny store?

But then the old woman who owned the store became sick. I kept her alive as long as I could, but I was so tiny, I could only just barely affect anything in the world.

When she died, I would die also. She was the last person anywhere that still believed in me. But then I heard the prayer of another. It was you, Ed, do you remember? For the first time in your life, you prayed and really meant it.

You said, "If anyone out there is listening, please make this sacrifice worth it. Please save my sister and my mother. I don't care about myself, but please let them live!"

Ed slammed on the brakes having wandered off listening to the story and allowing the car to reach near its top speed. As the Model-T screeched to a halt, he moved it to the side of the road. There was no other traffic, but he didn't want to have to worry about how long they were parked.

Once the car was entirely stopped, he turned it

off and got out, slamming the door and running a few dozen yards away from it.

Ed, what's wrong?

"No!" Ed shouted, allowing some real emotions to come to the surface.

I don't understand. No what, Ed?

"No!" He shouted as loud as he could back at the car. "No, you are not going to talk about that!" Ed was yelling at the car as if the vehicle and the voice were one and the same.

I have to explain everything to you. This is the most beautiful story. I know you don't understand why yet, but I am trying to tell you. I know you feel like you did the wrong thing, but you didn't! You were a glorious hero! You saved your sister and your mother! No one else IN THE WORLD could have done what you did. You were so brave!

"If you keep talking about it, I am not going to Crystal River. I will go back and work on the car and use the magnets and be rid of you forever!"

The voice was silent for a bit; Ed knew he still had some power over it.

You don't mean that, Ed. We're friends.

"Friends don't bring up memories from the past like that. Some things never happened. A real friend knows that."

A real friend helps even when it hurts. Sticks with

you through thick and thin. Helps you do the right thing and helps you when you don't know what the right thing is.

"I know what the right thing is! It is you who so often seems confused!"

I am going to finish my story, Ed. You have to know this; you have to understand so we can start the project. I have to help you stop thinking like a salesman and start thinking like a prophet. You are my prophet, Ed! What a splendid honor for you!

Ed stood resolute.

If you don't listen, I will come back early. And I will not be kind if we are no longer friends.

Ed's resolve wavered. A wind picked up from nowhere. Not a pleasant breeze, something darker. There was a hot edge to it.

If you don't listen, I will come back now, take your lungs, finish this time.

Ed's resolve was gone. He had endured tuberculosis, a horrific infliction. It had left him at the same time the voice started talking to him. She took credit for its regression, but Ed was never sure.

A deep sadness washed over him. He didn't know if he could hold it together if he had to remember. If he had to relive the moments that led to his escape from Russia all those years ago.

He fell to his knees. "Please don't make me

remember." Tears fell from his eyes; he put his head down with his hands on either knee.

Ed, you honor me with the pose of the priest! You are my prophet for sure! I always had faith in you, but how else could you know to prostrate yourself at just the right time? You are amazing! I can feel the power returning, and that's just with you! Just with one believer. But you are more than that now, aren't you?

The hot wind faded back to a pleasant November breeze.

Arise, my prophet, and receive your message.

Ed's will was gone; he stood back up and walked to the car, getting in and starting it. He sat on the side of the road for a few moments. He wasn't composing himself; he wasn't doing anything. He just didn't have the energy to lift his head and to pull forward.

After a bit longer, he looked up, released the brake, and started down the road again.

> *You said, "If anyone out there is listening, please make this sacrifice worth it. Please save my sister and my mother. I don't care about myself, but please let them live!"*
>
> *Those were the sweetest words I had ever heard. I have received millions of sacrifices, some so heartfelt and some so meaningless. But your words ended just*

as the old lady died. Without you, I would have passed too.

Instead, you sacrificed a baby to me, Ed! A sweet little baby! Your sister's baby! And you didn't do it for yourself; you did it for them!

Do you remember what I told you? I said, Edward, I am here, and I hear you. Do not fear; your sacrifice is not in vain.

At that moment, I was filled with the power, and I smote the soldiers searching for you! I took them right there, reaching in and separating their lives from their beating hearts.

Then you believed! You saved me!

And you still believe. I know you also think that I'm a carnival trick and a projection from some evil gypsy. That you can use magnets to detect who I really am and get rid of me. But that doesn't matter, because you also know what I did. You have seen the power I can have.

And you believe it. For as long as you live, you will know it. Because I am the truth!

Ed was sad. The voice had its say, but he knew that he had to correct the record to maintain his sanity. He had to get the words out into the world, so the truth existed next to the lie.

"I had nothing to do with the revolt. We were never political. But the soldiers, after Bloody Sunday, were rounding up anyone they thought *could* be a threat. Hanging them in the street, doing horrible things to the women. They killed my father and brother-in-law. We were all that was left, the four of us. We needed to escape to the countryside—my mother, my sister, and her new baby.

"We hid in the cellar. The soldiers were everywhere, but we were on the outskirts. If we could hide and wait until they left, we could make our escape.

"The baby wouldn't stop crying. He was hungry. My sister didn't have the resolve to do what needed to be done. I did. We stayed silent; the guards didn't find us. That night we made it out of Saint Petersburg. Alive!"

The car was rolling along on the bright Florida day. They were now well into the Everglades, past the farms and any type of modern civilization. Ed had driven this road a few times and knew a gas station was about halfway, plus a trading post run by the local Indian tribe. That station was probably still about an hour or hour and a half ahead.

Ed, you were a hero. If you had not prayed to me and had not sacrificed the child, you and your entire family would be dead now, your bloodline gone from the world forever.

"Maybe that would have been best!" Ed still had tears in his eyes, returning now as he grappled with his memories.

Silly! What's best is what we are about to do.

"My sister and mother disavowed me because I saved them! My mother spat my name and cursed me! She couldn't understand I had to sacrifice one to save many. The final time I ever heard her voice was to hear her wish me dead!"

Ed, I praise your name and revere you! You traded up!

EXCAVATION

NOVEMBER 17, 1919, 5 A.M.

There was a knock on the door.

Stone opened his eyes. His head hurt. His eyes hurt. There was blood everywhere.

Where the hell am I?

He put his hand up to his nose; fresh blood was seeping out.

He felt light-headed.

Knock. Knock. Knock. "Sheriff!"

The voice was that of Jorge Washington, one of Stone's deputies. Many of the Indians took different names to get their citizenship.

I'm back at home. How did I get here from the bar?

Knock. Knock. Knock. "Sheriff!"

"I'm asleep, Jorge!" Stone rolled out of bed, pulled his bloody undershirt off, throwing it in the corner. He put his head in a large water basin, rinsing the blood off and wetting his long greasy hair and white beard.

"They found a body at the excavation site."

Stone sat on the edge of the bed, using the dirty sheet to wipe the water off.

"Sheriff!"

"I heard you. Why would we care if they dug up a thousand-year-old body? What day is it?"

"It's a murder. It's a kid! From Miami City. We need you out there ASAP." A short pause. "It's Monday."

After Stone cleaned up, he pulled on a new undershirt. Looking back at his bed, it was a bloody mess. There was a lot of blood. If it was all his, he would have to be careful. If it wasn't, he would need to figure out what happened.

"Hold on," Stone said as he opened the door to the small shack that he lived in, pushed past Washington, heading straight for the outhouse. Once inside, he closed the door and threw up, wondering what he could have eaten. After a few more moments of using the outhouse for what it was meant for, he reemerged, walking past Washington and back into the dilapidated structure.

He brushed his teeth with Colgate and a new toothbrush he bought a couple days ago. When done, he put on his sheriff shirt, wiped his face and mouth again with the clean parts of the sheets from the bed, slicked his hair back under his round wide-brim official hat, and exited the door.

"You want a Coca-Cola?" Stone asked Washington as he walked past him again and over to the slow-running canal on his property. He needed a boost to try and alleviate the headache and his general feeling of terribleness.

"No, Sherriff, I'm a coffee drinker," Washington said as he put his hat back on and followed Stone to the water.

Stone walked out over a short, poorly built wood pier and pulled up a rope. The rope was tied around a crate. Stone pulled it onto the pier and opened it. Inside were eight bottles of Coca-Cola. Stone took two bottles out, sealed the box, and lowered it back down into the water. He used his long hunting knife to pop the top off one of the bottles and took a long pull.

The beverage was cool and crisp. Delicious. Instantly Stone could feel the energy and calming of the sugar and narcotic taking the edge off of things while giving him focus and liveliness.

"That stuff is gonna kill you, Judge," Washington said, using Stone's nickname as everyone did.

"'Thirst Knows No Season,' Jorge. None at all," Stone returned, using Coke's current marketing slogan, tipping the bottle at Washington, finishing it, then popping the top off the second one. He threw the first bottle into the canal.

Washington watched the bottle splash in the water. "There should be a law against littering, Judge."

"Should be lots of things, Jorge." Stone took a sip from the second bottle. He would take his time and enjoy this one.

They walked over to Washington's police car. Citrus County had money but not an unlimited supply. They funded fifteen hundred dollars for the sheriff's department to purchase vehicles. Stone made the decision. They could have gotten two nice enclosed cars or three of the bottom of the line five-hundred dollars each model. A roof but no side enclosures. No windshield.

Stone, of course, got three. With eight deputies running two shifts a day, he could always have two vehicles out and about and still keep one back at the office for an emergency.

The two got in the car, Washington driving. As they pulled away, it took a few moments to drive out of the orange grove that Stone lived behind, Stone started to consider what Jorge had said. Citrus County was almost a thousand square miles of orange groves. The biggest producer of oranges in the world. Phosphate mining was catching on also, making Citrus County an economic leader in the state.

Stone finished the second soda and tossed the bottle into the grove. "So what's this about murder, Jorge? How do we know it isn't natural causes? Those damn college kids up there digging holes to nowhere, getting drunk and partying."

Washington kept his eyes on the dirt road. "Not this one, Judge. This is some grizzly shit. It's good you don't have any breakfast down; you would lose it quickly."

"I seen a lot, Jorge. More than most."

"I know it, Judge. I don't follow and respect you because of your outward charisma." Jorge glanced over to suggest the opposite to Stone. "We all know who you are, what you done. We all know you know what's what and that you got our backs. Not that we don't wish, from time to time, you consider a bath every now and then." He wasn't smiling; it wasn't a joke.

"From your lips to God's ears," Stone said back, not smiling either.

Washington continued, focusing back on the crime. "It looks like some kind of ritual. Sick stuff. I ain't never heard about nothing like it. Never read anything like it in a book either."

Stone was getting curious. Washington was a man's man—young, tall, and good-looking for an Indian. He was respected among his people and

Stone's.

Stone put a finger to one side of his nose and blew snot and blood out, then the other. There was still a tiny trickle of blood running from his nose down the back of his throat, but it was almost all stopped.

Washington made a face of disgust. "Whatever you are doing to yourself, Judge, you need to start doing something else. We have a medicine woman on the reservation. After we get done at Crystal River, I am going to take you to go see her."

Stone looked over at Washington sideways but didn't argue, making a face instead.

He knew he was in a bad place now and that a real Indian medicine man, or woman, probably could help him. It wouldn't be the first time. He knew he would have to go through the painful process of them discovering some of his demons, but it was perhaps necessary now. And, if Washington were this bold about it, then it was probably long overdue.

"So how do you know the victim is from Miami City?" Stone asked, changing the subject back.

"He was wearing a letter from a high school on his jacket. We called a few hours ago and got a response before I came out to get you. It's confirmed. Dade is contacting his family. The officer on watch we talked to actually knew of the kid. He is a starting varsity pitcher for Miami

Senior High. He apparently is—well, *was*—pretty good. Named Eric Adams."

They didn't talk for the rest of the drive, a comfortable silence shared many times before.

The site they were heading to was under excavation by academics from Florida State University out of Tallahassee. Stone had been there several times, helping the county with the permit and conducting periodic checks to ensure everything was in order. The dig was big money and could be big news, changing the academic understanding of Florida's history.

They had discovered several buildings on the shores of Crystal River that were thousands of years old. The local Indians said they were built by the rubber people from another land. Washington had explained that the rubber people were the pre-Myan of Central America. Finding ancient settlements in Florida would be a significant and meaningful find for sure.

While that was interesting, the real discovery took place just a year ago. A large hill on an island right offshore, maybe a hundred feet away from the main settlement. It was a huge hill that turned out to be a pyramid. They just started uncovering it a few months ago. Stone had not checked in since then, so he was interested to see what might have been found.

They eventually pulled up to the primary dig

site. There were maybe thirty people, mostly college students from the look of it, and a few others too. No one was working; instead, the whole group was standing on the shoreline, looking over to the island. There was a small boat on the island's small beach. However, whatever was going on over there, you could not see it from here.

Stone got out of the car and walked to the beach, pushing through the crowd. There was no other boat or way over. He turned to Washington and nodded his head, indicating Washington and the boat on the opposite shore.

Washington nodded, then yelled, cupping his hands to project his voice over the hundred feet of water. He yelled a few times. Finally, a man wearing blue overalls exited the foliage, waved, and got in the boat to bring it over.

"Is that Pete or Stu? I can't tell," Stone said to Washington as they watched the man rowing the boat towards them.

"That's Pete. I thought everyone knew. Stu got eaten by an alligator about a month ago."

Stone looked at him to make sure he was serious. "Really? I should have been told that."

Washington looked Stone in the eye, turning his head to do so. "Judge, I'm pretty sure you were," he said, dropping eye contact and turning his head back to watch Pete row the boat.

Stone continued to stare at Washington's ear for a few beats, then looked back at the boat as it slowly approached.

When the boat arrived, Stone could see that Pete was worked up. As soon as it hit the white sand, Pete frantically started motioning for Stone and Washington to get in.

"Sherriff, we're all glad you're here! Come on now, hurry up. You gotta find who did this. It's a horror! Someone tied that boy up and bit off his privates! Hurry up now!"

Stone and Washington exchanged glances. "Jorge, stay here and get everyone's name and a way to contact them. A few gawkers don't look like college students; that guy in the suit, for example. Keep anyone that you think is interesting here until I get back; we can interrogate them then."

Washington nodded as Pete pushed the boat back and started rowing as fast as his old arms could.

"Did you find the body?" Stone asked.

"No, one of them poindexters digging all the holes found him. You should have seen them all, running around, crying, in a panic. They all get here at 2 a.m. The second shift gets more work done before it gets too hot."

Stone looked at Pete. "You the resident groundskeeper?"

"Yep."

"You see anyone suspicious?"

"Nope. I sleep between 7 p.m. when the first shift leaves and 2 a.m. when the second shift gets here. I didn't see nothing."

Stone nodded and looked back up to the approaching island.

"Don't you want to hear about what got done to this boy?"

"I got eyes, Pete. I don't need no secondhand exposition."

Pete snorted and rowed harder.

When the boat beached on the island, Stone waited for Pete to get out and pull it past the waterline. He didn't want to get his shoes wet. "Pete, stay here with the boat. I don't care if President Woodrow Wilson himself is over there waving his arms and calling for you. You stay here until I tell you differently, got it?"

Stone could sometimes talk with a lot of authority, and his deep bass voice suggested Pete should do as he said. Pete nodded that he understood, probably not expecting Woodrow Wilson to show up anyway.

The island was small but very overgrown. The hill was pretty tall, seven or eight stories total if it had been a building. Not a skyscraper-in-a-big-city tall, but certainly Florida-in-the-middle-of-nowhere tall. A path had been cleared, presumably by the excavation team. Stone followed it; within a step or two, he went from island beach to being completely surrounded by foliage and no view of the large, fast-moving river.

He worked his way along the path slowly, looking here and there for anything out of the ordinary, not seeing anything. The trail wound around the hill a couple times. Upon finally reaching the top. There were three people standing around, an older man and two pretty girls, probably in their early twenties.

Isn't that always the way with these academics? Stone thought. The graduate students for these old guys always seemed to fit a very specific mold.

The two students were standing well away from the body, clearly shaken up. The man was standing closer but with his back to the scene, almost as though he were guarding it. When he saw Stone come over the rise, the man started walking to him, putting his hand out to shake Stone's in greeting.

"Sheriff, thank God you are here." They shook hands. "I'm Professor Goldman; this is my dig. I sent a runner to your office when the scene was discovered."

"Did you find the body?" Stone asked.

"No, those two over there did. Mary and Helen. They run the second shift. This is their final semester; they will both graduate in a month with their master's degrees."

"Stone kept his eyes on Goldman. "Has anything been disturbed?"

Goldman looked surprised. "No! You will understand when you see it. Well, yes. Anyone that has seen the body has vomited. That would be me, Mary, Helen, and Pete, the groundskeeper."

"Professor. I need you to stand right here and don't do anything for a bit. Don't try and help me look around. Don't interject when I interview the girls. I know what I'm doing and don't need their testimony prompted trying to impress you."

A look of indignation flashed across Goldman's face. It quickly faded; he nodded his understanding to the gravity of the situation.

Stone nodded back and walked over to the bloody scene. It was gruesome like he had been told. The boy had been tied down, one post high above his head and the other low below his feet. There were bite marks all over, deep ones taking out chunks of flesh. The most apparent wound was below his waist, the marks culminating around his private area, which had been wholly bitten away, now just a mangled void where most of his body fluid had ultimately escaped.

The bite marks were smallish, not the size of a full-grown adult, not that of a child either.

Could other teenagers have done this? What the hell is wrong with people today?

Stone looked at the rope around the boy's hands and feet. There was a lot of scoring and rope-burning. He had struggled mightily.

Dear God, he was bitten to death, and they ate off his privates while he was still alive?

The horror of the scene washed over Stone. He felt sick and quickly moved away, vomiting. When he was done, he turned back at Goldman, whose face was a combination of sympathy and an "I told you so" look.

Stone took his outer sheriff shirt off and laid it over the lower portion of the body. He stood there in his clean white undershirt, looking down. The sun was rising in the east. Its bright morning rays perfectly intersected the hill they were on, shining into the recessed top of the structure where the boy had been tied up at the perfect angle. Stone realized the area under the body was a rectangle, with its top pointing to the rising sun.

Stone's white shirt seemed to glow in the morning light as he stood studying the scene.

There was something in the boy's mouth. Stone paused to gather himself, then bent down, using his hand to push the jaw open so he could see inside.

A bolt had been inserted under the jaw from the

outside, driven through the chin and tongue. A top nut was screwed in, seemingly there to keep the tongue in place.

He could have produced screams but no words or inflections. Diabolical.

Stone studied things for a bit longer, ensuring he had the image in his head in case he needed to remember it later. He had about half an hour to see how things were going to go now that he had seen the body. He didn't ever wish for an attachment, but sometimes it made the job easier. An attachment was an earthbound spirit who followed Stone around, usually hoping Stone could help them resolve something related to their death.

Turning, he walked over to the two grad students, Mary and Helen. Both clearly had been crying and still looked spooked.

As soon as Stone approached, the taller of the two said, "Sheriff! Can you believe it! Did you see what they did to him?" Witnesses like this almost always wanted to talk about what they had seen. The problem was, they were looking at the horror and spectacle, which Stone could see for himself. He needed to know if they had seen anything timely, no longer present or evident.

"Did either of you see anything this morning when you arrived? Did you notice anything out of the ordinary?"

The two looked at each other; they had clearly been discussing the whole situation for some time now between themselves. The taller one spoke again. "We didn't notice anything, Sheriff, until we got up here. It was a bit darker than usual, but that was it."

"Did you see anyone? Hear a horse? Hear a car?"

"No, but honestly, we weren't listening for anything either. We were talking like we always do on the trip over."

Stone looked around, then looked back. It seemed the shorter girl, the one who had not spoken yet, had something she wanted to say.

Stone looked at her and asked, "Do you have anything to add, miss...?" as if suggesting she should let him know if she were Mary or Helen.

"I'm Mary, Sheriff. I just wanted to know." She was turning red in the face. "Do you think you will find it?"

"We will look for the perpetrator if that's what you mean. It is a gruesome crime. Whoever did this needs to be found, so they don't do it again."

She looked unconvinced. "No, Sheriff, I mean... You know. Do you think his thing is still around here?"

Good Christ, she wants to know about his privates. What the hell is wrong with kids these days?

"I doubt it, young miss. But if we do, I'll make

sure you are the first person I alert."

***

I should have left ten minutes ago.

Yes, you should have.

"I'm going to need to think, Voice. You need to honor our deal and leave me alone for a while."

You're going to need me, Ed. I can tell you things that will get you off the hook. Tell them the truth. Tell them you are here on your retirement, interested in donating to the university's archeology department. It will explain everything.

"How could you know how a university works or what the police want to hear?"

But it was a good idea; he was wealthy, after all. Worth over a million dollars. He could easily prove it to a local sheriff. He could explain his retirement, the land he was planning on purchasing, and claim he was looking to offer an endowment. That was what rich people did anyway. Why not him too?

Ed watched the two law enforcement officers arrive. One of the men looked like a hard man, rugged and rough around the edges. He seemed to be in charge, getting into the small rowboat and taken over to the island.

The other man was a tall, good-looking Indian. He was clearly the deputy, calling out in an authoritative voice to all the people gathered on this side of the river.

The deputy worked his way through the large group of people, eventually getting to Ed. "Sir, may I have your name and occupation, please?" he asked. He had asked the same question to twenty-nine other people, but it came out fresh, and he seemed interested.

Did he save me for last for a reason?

Of course, he did; you're the only person wearing a business suit!

Shut up, shut up, shut up! I have to be able to think.

I'm telling you, Ed, I'm gonna help.

"Sir?"

Ed realized he had been standing there with his mouth open, focused on his internal dialog. "Sorry, officer. What was the question?"

"I'm a deputy, not an officer. I need your name and occupation, please."

Tell him the truth.

Shut up, you!

"My name is Ed Leeds. I'm retired. I just retired last week on Friday!"

The deputy looked at him, making a note in his notebook with a rounded dull pencil.

"Well, congratulations, sir, on your retirement. What did you retire from?"

Ed's face lit up. "I sold Carrier air conditioners! They are top-of-the-line units. I still have connections if you are interested in something for your police station! It makes the days pass pleasantly and the nights more enjoyable."

The deputy smiled at him. "We are the county sheriff's office, sir, not a police station."

Ed, what the hell are you doing?

Voice, I've been selling these things for half a decade without you. I know what I am doing.

Ed, you know my name now. Use it.

"Sir?"

Ed realized he had drifted off again into his own thoughts. The voice was so distracting.

"Yes?" He recovered, sounding salesman-like, getting confused about which conversation he was in, as the voice often did to him.

"I asked you why you are at an archeological dig so early in the morning?"

He asked you why you are at an archeological dig so early in the morning.

Ya, thanks. I heard him this time.

"It's a funny story, actually, officer. I came here to inspect the progress. I am in the process of purchasing land near Miami City, and I am considering an endowment to the state university."

The deputy made a face at the word officer, then just stared at Ed for a while.

It made Ed a little nervous.

Ed tried smiling, then looking away. Looking back. Looking serious.

"Sir, can I see your hands, please." It wasn't a question.

Ed, don't show him! It's a trap. He suspects you.

Thanks, Voice. I figured that out on my own.

IX-Chel! Use my name! It gives me power, which I can use to help you!

Ed put his hands out between himself and the deputy.

Ed was a small man, and he had small hands. But they were rough and well weathered. Callused here and there from years of manual labor in Russia. Otherwise, they were clean and unremarkable.

The deputy turned them over, looking for something that he apparently did not find.

"You haven't asked me what happened. All the other people I have talked to here on the beach asked me if I knew any more about what was going on."

Ed could tell the Indian was suspicious of something. He had no idea what it could be.

"Why would I ask you if you knew what was

going on? I watched you walk over. The other fella got on the boat and hasn't come back yet. I suspect you know about as much as I do. I got here after they found the body, and I have heard all the kids describing what they saw."

Brilliant Ed. I'm quiet for thirty seconds, and you impress the heck out of me.

Please, please, please shut up. I can't tell if those are my thoughts or yours. I have to talk straight to this guy, or we're never going to get out of here.

I'm just trying to provide you moral support.

"Sir?"

Oh no, I didn't hear what he said, did you?

No, you were yelling at me for trying to help you.

"Yes?" Ed smiled.

"Sir, I am going to need you to stay here until the sheriff comes back over. Can you do that?"

"Why?"

Apparently, that was the straw that broke the camel's back; the deputy's face turned angry. He took a pair of handcuffs off his belt and put them on Ed's wrists while Ed stood there watching.

See what you made happen! If I could have just thought for myself, everything would have been fine.

Yep, Ed, you were right. You're in a pickle now, sure enough. That whole conversation was a wooden nickel.

SHERIFF'S OFFICE

NOVEMBER 17, 1919, 1 P.M.

Jorge Washington put the phone receiver back into the handle, ending the call. He looked over to the other deputy on duty, Bonaparte "Bone" Mizell. Mizell was a tall, lanky cracker who often thought it was funny to call Jorge Apple, red on the outside and white on the inside. When he did, Jorge would call him Milk Toast, referring to a cracker that was all wet: Mizell, Milk Toast; it almost rhymed.

"Bone," Washington said, looking over, "Miami is all set to receive the body. Did you get the flight coordinated?"

Mizell looked back, finding a notepad on his desk and flipping a few pages. "Yes, they can take him on the plane Friday afternoon. That is the next flight.

Washington made a face. "I think that's too long. That body is already starting to reek. Let me see if Dade can talk to the parents. Get their permission to have our mortician prepare it on this side instead of waiting for the family's choice to do it."

Mizell shrugged and looked over to Ed, who was asleep on a cot in one of the two holding cells. "You don't really think that scrawny little dude has anything to do with this, do you?"

Washington was halfway to picking the phone back up to make another call. He paused. "I'll let the sheriff figure it out; that's his specialty. The little guy was sure acting weird, and he is from Miami City, just like the boy. Certainly worth some time to study on it."

Mizell snorted his disbelief.

After a few more calls, Washington had it all worked out. Everyone was fine with the Citrus County morgue preparing the body for transport. This included embalming it using formaldehyde to reduce the decay process, and the most important thing, to reduce the otherwise overwhelming stench of death.

"Where's the sheriff?" Mizell asked after a few moments of silence.

"He stayed to oversee the removal of the body. He is also searching this fella's car for anything suspicious, then he'll drive it back here to the station when everything there is in a bow."

Mizell smiled. "This fella here knows Stone's gonna drive his car? Stone ain't exactly a triple-A Grand Prix winner behind the wheel. The sheriff is more comfortable on a horse than in a motorized vehicle."

Washington smiled. "You ever gone with him where he drove?"

"Once. One time. Never felt less in control and fearful for my life than those twenty minutes. I made him pull over so I could drive the rest of the way."

"Smart man, Milk Toast."

"Said Apple."

***

Judge Stone walked around Ed's car, looking at it for any sign of a struggle, blood, tools, marks in the dirt around it, anything that could have been used to abduct the boy or transport him. Stone didn't see how small Ed Leeds could have overpowered Eric Adams, the dead boy. The kid had a big frame and was clearly a top high school athlete in good physical condition.

It had been almost six hours since Stone saw the body, and nothing had shown up yet. No disembodied voices or full-body apportions. No cryptic messages from the dead pleading with Stone to help with this, to bring closure to that.

Still, it wasn't all done like clockwork. He knew

enough about death, and life, to understand that every situation was different.

The car checked out fine. It was clean and well kept, but not too clean. It hadn't been wiped down recently. There was road and travel dirt and grime on it, but not an excessive amount. There was no visible blood, no torn seats. No tools or ropes or anything other than Ed's travel bag and a few changes of clothes.

Stone looked up to the sky; it was getting on past midday, probably now one-thirty or two o'clock. Everything was done here, and everyone had left. The body was with the county people. He walked around the car a few more times, then decided to walk the island one more time, now that the sun was at a different angle. Better to be safe than sorry.

The small boat was tied up on the beach. Stone walked over to it, untied it, and rowed himself over to the island. The current was strong. When he got to the island, he pulled the boat all the way onto the small short beach, several feet up out of the water, the front of the boat resting in the foliage.

He started the trail to the top of the hill, looking closely at the ground and surroundings. So many people had now traversed the area he doubted he would find anything. He tried to remember back to what the dirt path looked like when he had first arrived. It looked about like it looked now, honestly.

There were no drag marks this morning or now. Whoever murdered Eric either carried him up the hill or made him walk. If Eric had been made to walk to his death, it implied someone strong enough to control the big kid. Certainly not Ed Leeds.

As Stone rounded the top of the hill, he saw a tall, strong-looking young man standing, looking at the still bloody spot where Eric's body had been. Stone knew who it was right away, and slight disappointment passed over him. There were several types of spirits. Stone knew because he was one himself, returned to the living on a bad deal that he had grown to regret over a very long time.

He hadn't always regretted it, and there were moments, still, where even though it was a bad deal, that didn't mean it wasn't good for him. But the gaps between the good parts and the bad parts were getting more expansive.

In any event, what Stone saw before him, he knew, was the earthbound spirit of Eric Adams. This was a lower type of manifestation. Stone would be able to talk to Eric, but Eric wouldn't know too much. Not like a full-reborn ethereal who had a command of time and space. Spirits like Maggie and Jack.

"Hello, son," Stone said, slowly approaching the spirit.

Eric turned. "Sheriff! Thank goodness you are here! I think something happened. Look at all the blood. There should be a body here, I think, but I can't find it."

"We moved the body, Eric. We can't leave it here; this isn't a cemetery."

Eric was wearing the clothes he had been killed in. Blue jeans, a green t-shirt, and his high school varsity letter jacket.

Stone knew not to spook the spirit. He needed to talk to Eric and find out as much as he could about what happened. He already knew what Eric required from him. Unlike how this often went, this time, Stone would be able to provide closure to Eric's spirit with only a few simple actions that would happen anyway, with or without Stone's involvement.

"Eric, do you remember what happened?"

Eric looked back down to where his body had been. "I know something terrible happened, Sheriff, but I don't remember."

"What is the last thing you do remember, Eric?" Stone was slowly advancing. Nothing threatening, just to get closer, so he did not have to raise his voice so much in the conversation.

"It's gonna sound weird, sir. There was a big serpent with feathers. It talked in a sexy voice. It was a woman! She was so beautiful, some kind of

Indian. Not the kind from around here, the kind from Mexico. We, you know, hit it off."

Stone knew.

"What were you doing over here on the Gulf Coast from Miami City?"

Eric looked at him, becoming a little unsure. He faded in and out for a moment, flashing between the clean-cut varsity letter wearer to his mangled and bloody final form.

Slow it down, Stone. These manifestations are fragile and might flee or give up.

Eric stabilized. "That's all I remember. I know I am supposed to stay with myself. I need to go home, but I don't know what that means. And I can't find myself. Do you understand?"

"Yes, I understand, Eric. I'm here to help. I'm the county sheriff. I came here to take you home. Can you trust me?"

Eric looked at Stone for a long time, studying him, also reacting to something else. Finally, "Yes, sir. They are all, everyone, telling me to trust you. I would anyway, I think. I need your help."

"Good, Eric. Here is what I need you to do. Look at me closely. See the light?"

"Yes, sir."

"It's not that bright, but it is like the light you need to find. When you see the brighter light, go to it. In the meantime, stay with me, follow my light, and you will be fine. I'll guide you there. We have to take your body back home. I know where both are, your body and your home. When we are all together and all home, you will know what to do."

***

Ed was awakened by a clattering on the cell bars.

Jorge Washington, the Indian deputy that had arrested him, was running a spoon back and forth on the side of the cell.

Ed had been in a deep sleep; it took him a moment to remember where he was. He sat up on the edge of the narrow cot, shaking his head to try and hurry the process along.

"Mr. Leeds, do you need to use the facilities?"

Ed realized that he indeed did. He nodded, picked up his suit coat, and stood up.

"Please stand back from the door. Okay, follow me. When you are finished, you're going to talk to Sheriff Stone."

It was said in such a way that it sounded like Ed had an appointment with the president.

Washington led him to an indoor bathroom. When he was finished in the bathroom they walked back to the front, past the two holding cells, heading out onto the street.

Ed stopped. "I thought you wanted me to talk to

the sheriff?"

"The sheriff can be a bit unconventional, Mr. Leeds."

What does that mean?

Shut up, you. I am serious. Let me talk to this guy and get the heck out of here. I didn't get to see whatever you were trying to show me at the Crystal River thing, so just let me get out of here. I am really, really serious. If you bug me, I am going to stop believing in you!

There was blessed silence in Ed's head.

Ed and the deputy walked together out into the mild November Florida afternoon. Still warming into the low eighties, but pleasant enough, hinting at even better weather to come. Washington turned right, then crossed the wide street, technically jay-walking, a new crime Citrus County just voted to put on the books, reacting to pressure from the auto industry.

The two continued down Second Avenue a few blocks, then turned and entered the Hound & Fox bar.

Stone was seated at a table booth in the back. There was no one else in the building.

"It opens in a couple hours. Sheriff Stone uses this place as a kind of private office. You go sit down and talk to him. I'm going to wait here by the door."

Ed waited a few moments for his eyes to adjust to the dark interior. There wasn't much light, but the building was cool and had good air ventilation. It wasn't air conditioning, though.

When we're done, I'll see if I can find the owner. A good Carrier unit could triple revenues here over the whole summer. It will pay for itself in under a year.

Then nothing. The voice was going to leave him alone. Fantastic.

Ed walked up to the man sitting in the back booth. The sheriff had an odd look about him, wearing his bright white undershirt instead of the sheriff shirt that Ed had seen him in earlier. Stone looked weathered, more so than his mid-thirties features would have suggested. He had dark hair with a salt-and-pepper beard. His eyes were piercing, a light blue that seemed to look right into your soul.

Stone didn't say anything as Ed approached. Ed waived hello awkwardly and sat down on the other side of the booth. Stone was facing the door; Ed now had his back to it.

"Mr. Leeds?" Stone said, his voice soft but deep. It carried the room, almost making the table between them vibrate.

"Yes, Sheriff?"

"Why were you at the archeological site this morning?"

Ed waited.

Nothing.

"I mentioned this to your deputy; I just retired last week. I'm in the process of buying some land in Florida City. I came up here because I am interested in archeology and the work the state university is doing. I wanted to see the site for myself as I consider providing the school an endowment to continue the work."

Stone looked at him, keeping eye contact.

The silence in the room grew loud. Ed started to get a little nervous.

"What is it about archeology that you find so interesting you would seek to give some money away to a state-funded school?"

Uh-oh.

"I've always been fascinated by the past."

The sheriff stared at him hard. "I'm more interested in the present."

What was your idea about what to say to get out of this?

Ed smiled.

Okay, I was kidding before. We need to get back and get to work. A little help would be appreciated.

Nothing.

"Mr. Leeds"—the sheriff had a look of

annoyance—"I need you to stay focused."

"I'm sorry, Sheriff. I think I am still in shock about what happened out there. About you finding that boy and what had been done to him. I keep thinking about it and losing my thoughts."

Ed decided to continue.

When in doubt, spell it out.

"I came to the United States from Russia, escaping their civil war. I did lots of jobs when I first got here. I was a tree logger for a while, but the work was too taxing for me.

"I don't have a problem with hard work, mind you. But I'm no Paul Bunyan. I couldn't keep up with the other fellas. You may not know this, but you get paid by the tree, so I wasn't making enough money.

"But I didn't quit either. I invented a new type of hand ax, one that was easier to use on the shimmy. I sold almost five hundred units until copies started showing up at a price below what I could make them for.

"I did a couple other things, then saw an air conditioner at the World's Fair in Knoxville. It was just the most fantastic contraption. It operated on the principle of separation. The idea was so simple once you understood it, but the ingenuity of it was just incredible.

"So, I started selling them. I would have been

happier working as an engineer for Carrier, but they already had everyone they needed. The product was largely done, although they continue to improve and refine it every year. The next big invention they have is centrifugal chillers. These are big machines. The plan is to be able to cool huge buildings by putting one on the roof. It should be ready in the next year or two. Part of me wants to go back when they have them ready for sale. Can you imagine the commission selling a huge building versus just someone's house or small business?"

The sheriff's expression had softened. He was listening intently to Ed's perception; more listening now than accusing.

"So anyway, I worked my way down and ended up in Miami City. What better place to be an air conditioning salesman than Miami City. I made good money, enough to retire and stop hustling.

"There is a plot of land, ten acres, just outside of Florida City, in Homestead County, that I am going to purchase and build my retirement home on."

Ed smiled his salesman smile as he finished.

Stone's expression changed to a quizzical look. "What county did you say?"

"Homestead County? They have the county seat there, right in Florida City. How lucky, right? And I know the mayor. He is helping me with the purchase since it is currently land owned by the incorporated town."

Ed could tell that Stone was deliberating something.

He probably doesn't have a bunch of voices in his head confusing him like I do. Lucky man.

"Mr. Leeds. I believe you."

Ed was relieved even though he had not realized he would be.

"But..." The sheriff seemed to have something on his mind. "Part of your story doesn't work for me. I think we do have a problem."

"It's the truth, Sheriff."

"I actually do believe that you think it is, Mr. Leeds."

"Can you call me Ed? Everyone calls me Ed."

"Ed. There is no such thing as Homestead County."

Ed wasn't expecting Stone to say that. It took him a moment to register.

"Sure there is. I have been there dozens of times. I was just there on Saturday, right in the main county administrative office."

"Where is this office?"

"I already told you, Florida City."

"And someone there is 'helping' you purchase land?"

"Yes, the mayor of Florida City also runs the county office." The tiniest of clicks happened for Ed. "Oh."

It would be odd for a city official to also be the primary administrator for a county, now that Ed thought about it. Everyone was so nice there, though; he had just accepted what they said at face value.

"Oh," Ed said again, "Sheriff, they said the land had to be sold at auction. The starting bid is going to be eighteen hundred dollars. Do you think this is a scam?"

"I've seen it before, Mr. Leeds. Ed. What will happen is one or probably two people you have never seen will show up. There will be a little drama; they will drive the bid price way up. You'll pay it because you'll be caught up in the moment. Then you will get a fake land deed, and suddenly in a day or two, the perpetrators will be gone, leaving you with nothing."

Ed paused, trying to take it all in. He had seen enough flimflam over the years. The more he thought about it, the more it made sense. Plus, Ed wasn't a saint by any stretch. He was a salesman and had run some gambits himself from time to time. Nothing at such an extreme level as this land scam, but small little griffs to get by or sell more.

"I need to purchase that land," he said back to Stone a little desperately, realizing that getting the land was the most important thing to him at the end of the day. He had to be able to build the machine to expel the voice, even if he could not think about it for fear of the voice discovering his actual plan. But the land location was the key.

Stone seemed to be thinking also. "Ed, do you have the parcel number for the lot you want to purchase?"

"Yes, of course." Ed had it on the paper Mayor Laundry had given him. The paper was in his car. "I have some paperwork in my car with the parcel number. Wait, Sheriff, the parcel number was given to me by Mayor Laundry. What if it isn't the right number?"

"Mr. Leeds. I am releasing you. You are still of interest to me in this ongoing murder investigation. But I don't think you did it, and I am not sure you have any other information I might need. However, that could change."

Stone continued. "I'm not the Dade sheriff, so what sounds like a criminal enterprise running a lot-ball scam is out of my jurisdiction.

"However, two things.

"First, I will be down to Miami City with the boy's body on Friday, in four days. While I am there, if you want, I can come to meet the players in this land deal. I won't be law enforcement; this isn't in my jurisdiction. But that doesn't mean I am the type to sit by and let grifters operate.

"Second, if you like, you can go to the Citrus County office here, tell them Sheriff Stone sent you. Have them pull the maps and verify the plot and parcel numbers for you. They should have records on who owns it too. Then you can look the actual owners up and work your deal directly with them.

"I'll alert the Dade sheriff of your situation and what you told me. I suggest you stop by and see them also when you get back, but that's not an official suggestion as sheriff, you understand."

MEDICINE

NOVEMBER 17, 1919, 10 P.M.

"She isn't your traditional medicine woman," Washington said as he drove the county patrol car through the fresh night air.

Stone looked over at him, then back to the road ahead.

"She's read the Bible, Judge. She believes it. She also knows the old ways, and she believes in those too."

"Wouldn't work if she didn't," Stone said, keeping his eyes forward. "Jorge, if this lady is what you say she is, we both know that I will be unavailable for a couple days. I've done the purge before, both guided and unguided. It's time, and it's been a while."

"It's time, Judge, that's for sure. And she is what I say she is."

They drove along in silence for a bit.

"Jorge, you take the lead on investigating the murder. When I head down to Miami City with the boy's body, I'll work that end of it. Figure out who this kid was, what circles he moved in. But that's ancillary at this point until you run everything to ground here. We don't know what we don't know right now."

Nodding, he replied, "I'm not entirely sure what to do, Judge, on this end."

"You got your list with all the names of the people?"

"Yes."

"Make sure you include the two graduate students, Mary and Helen. And Professor Goldman. That's thirty-some people. Follow up with each one individually. Have them come into the office if that helps. Get them talking, have Bone take good notes so you can focus on the interviews. Once all that's done, compare everything they said this morning and what they said in the interviews. Organize everything into things they all said and things only some said. Then do it again, only this time fill in the blanks. Follow up with any new leads. Verify any parts of their stories if they sound wonky. It will either start to paint a picture, or it won't. I'll stay in contact. I can't imagine I'll be down there for more than a week."

They were well down a small narrow dirt road, seven or eight miles inland from Crystal River.

"This ain't much of a reservation, Jorge," Stone noted, given the complete lack of any structures or people.

"We're going to see the three sisters. They are young and easy on the eyes but stay formal with them. They can be mean, vengeful bitches when they want to be."

Stone snapped as a thought hit him. He put his hands where the pockets on his sheriff shirt would typically be, but he was still just wearing his undershirt. "Jorge, what do I pay them with? I didn't bring anything for barter. I think I have maybe a dollar in change on me, nothing else."

Jorge smiled. "These are the three sisters, Judge. They are also my sisters. I vouched for you. Yes, they will want payment, though. I assured them already that you are good for it. I told them that this will be a hard one, a lot of work. That they can set their price at the end."

Stone nodded. He smirked to himself. *They will want a lot in exchange when this is all over.*

The road winded here and there amongst the palmetto bushes and palm trees. The dirt was turning to white sand in places, slowing the progress of the car and its skinny tires. Palmettos were a bush only in the most generic sense of the word. Short, broad, evil, thorny plants that grew like weeds all over Florida. They had a shallow root system and evolved into palm trees after a bit.

Stone could eventually see a fire through the trees. It would come and go from his view as the car meandered around the trail leading to their destination, turning almost randomly as they ultimately approached.

Washington stopped the car at the edge of the clearing. There were several huts made from the palmetto palms. The fire was generally in the center of things. A pinewood and rock structure was on one side. Stone knew this would be the lodge. Three figures were standing on this side of the fire, silhouetted against the orange and yellow flames. Presumably, this would be the three sisters, seeing the car lights and hearing the motor as Stone and Washington approached.

With the car stopped, Washington pulled up on the hand brake, engaging it.

"Here we go, Judge."

Washington led the way; Stone followed. As they grew near, Stone could make out the details of the three women; they were identical triplets.

"Triplets," he said to Washington in a low voice before they were in earshot.

"Quadruplets," Washington grinned and looked at Stone sideways.

"No kidding."

The three women had beautiful features. If Washington were good-looking, his sisters were stunning. Thin, tall, perfectly symmetrical qualities. They were dressed in one-piece flowing white robes, the fire behind them eliminating some of the robe's properties.

"Sheriff, please meet Elizabeth, Alice, and Martha." Washington stopped a few feet short, so Stone could advance and take center stage.

Knowing well the blended customs of the American Indian, Stone walked close and extended his hand, shaking the hand of each of the women in turn. In the current mixed society, the courtesy of a handshake would often not be offered to an Indian woman. Stone had lived with the Kiowa near Colorado for several years and understood how important traditions, and breaking them, could be.

The middle sister stepped close to Stone. The other two produced some type of plant from somewhere and started using it to trace Stone's outline, a few inches away as they moved it around him.

"Sheriff?" Martha, the sister in the center, said to him. Her voice was low and feminine, but she still sounded more like Deputy Washington than Stone expected. "Do you know your spirit name?"

Stone knew this was a qualifying question. Half of the Indian rituals were designed just to allow a person to learn their true name. But he knew his already; he had for a long time.

"Judge," he returned.

"Yes!" Martha's eyes became wide with interest. "Di-gu-go-di-s-gi!" she said loudly and slowly, emphasizing each syllable.

Stone knew the name, but she spoke in Cherokee, not Miccosukee.

"Yes, how did you know I learned the name in Cherokee?"

There were many Indian languages, not all related. The Cherokee were dominant in the West, not here in Florida. Here the Seminole reigned.

"One of your spirits told me."

Stone smiled, throwing her off.

"Which one?"

Martha's face lit up into a huge smile. "Jack."

Stone nodded. "Yep. Jack's easy to deal with; he has been through a lot with me. He knows what to do. I will tell you, though, I have another spirit with me now, a boy. Well, young man, I suppose. Eric Adams. I cannot risk losing him. I am taking his body to rest in Miami City on Friday. To rest with his family. If I lose him, he will wonder."

Martha looked deep into Stone's eyes. The other two sisters were finished with the plant ritual and stood back at Martha's side.

The fire crackled, the night grew darker, locked in its eternal struggle with the flames.

The sisters started whispering to each other, looking Stone up and down. Finally, after a good amount of looking and discussion, Martha said, "Your soul is pure and does not need cleansing. This means the spirits with you have no fear."

She stepped in, almost pressed against him. "However, your body is poisoned. If you were an ordinary man, you would be dead by now."

She made a face as if she immediately regretted her word choice.

Stone smiled, not stepping away, enjoying her closeness.

She smiled back without any joy in it. "Well, you know what I mean."

RETURN TRIP

NOVEMBER 18, 1919, 9 A.M.

Some weather was blowing across the state. A cold front was passing through. In the summer months, it would have brought a lot of rain. It did not bring rain currently, but the day was gloomy; a heavy mist hung in the air late into the morning. Little direct sunlight made its way through the cloud cover.

Ed had driven yesterday to the south of Tampa, then slept in the car, rejoining the trip home at first light. He was nearing Naples now. If everything went well, he could be back in Florida City by nightfall.

Do I really want to go back to Florida City, given what I learned?

Good morning, Edward.

Ed had been free of the voice for the past eighteen hours or so, ever since he met with the sheriff. He was startled by it showing back up. Then realized it was speaking differently with him, no longer professing its love for him as its opening statement.

"Voice, er, Seashell," he said, phonetically pronouncing the name, "you abandoned me yesterday when I needed you."

The world is a big place, Edward. I can't spend all my time with just one person.

Every warning alarm in Ed's head that could go off went off. Ed's entire plan could be in jeopardy if the voice found another person who believed in it. The whole world could be in trouble. He couldn't allow himself any of these thoughts while the voice was with him.

"Do you know what the sheriff told me?"

He still didn't entirely understand how the voice worked, how it knew some things and not others. How it could interact with him, but not always understand his true intentions.

Edward. You said you would help me with my project. Yet, as I remember, you have stalled and maneuvered to delay me by several years. You put building your castle before my needs, claiming they were intertwined. That we needed a special place to start the work.

But I know you believe you can use your castle to expose me and to banish me. You made those plans before you learned to hide some of your true thoughts from me. I let it all go because you are wrong; your silly plan to use magnets and electricity is ridiculous.

But Ed, I found someone else who believes!

Some of the old joy crept back into the voice.

Someone with followers of their own! We talked for a long time, and they have agreed to introduce me to their flock! Can you imagine! After all this time!

Ed went cold. He could imagine. He had to allow his subconscious to guide the conversation. If he tried to work it through in his head, the voice would hear.

"That's wonderful, IX-Chel." He made sure to say her name with the slightly different inflection from Seashell, even though it really did sound ninety-nine percent like Seashell, except the S's were softer and had a slight Z'ness to them, and there was a strong emphasis on the second syllable CH.

"Will they be helping me build the castle?"

Edward.

The familiarity was gone again.

My new flock already has a cathedral. Yes, it was built for another god. But no one there believes, not even the pastor! They want to believe! They are desperate to believe in something. With just a few of them, I can perform miracles. Miracles will create more believers.

The glorious circle will begin again!

"Does this mean you no longer need to start separating people into parts?"

No longer need to? Edward, Ed, it means the opposite! It means we can get started and begin the process of purging the world into the best parts of the true believers!

Ed did everything he could to keep any negative thoughts out of his head. He had learned that the voice could hear his primary thoughts, which sounded like words, where he was talking to himself in his head. But it could not pick up on emotions, feelings, or his subconscious. At least if it could, it had never hinted at it or produced any knowledge from it.

"What was it you wanted to show me at Crystal River?"

Oh, Ed, I loved you so much back then. Yesterday was such a different world than today!

I wanted you to see where I came from, to get to know me better. The Crystal River site is how I made it to this land. My original people came two thousand years ago. Can you comprehend how much time has passed?

They were great builders, and they all believed for so long. They understood the project; they helped me separate millions of people into their better parts. It was so glorious!

Ed thought he knew what separating meant. He knew some of the histories of Central and South America, enough to know the Mayans were very advanced but also very brutal. They sacrificed millions of people, cutting out their still-beating hearts, as the victims watched, screaming and pleading for their life, in agonizing pain. The Maya considered a ritual sacrifice perfect when they could get the heart out and up in front of the person with enough time for them to react to seeing their own heart still beating outside their body.

But Ed, my love, I made a mistake. I am willing to admit it. It wasn't until I traveled the world, in that last moment before I was gone, as the old woman died in the souvenir shop. It was your call that pulled me across the planet. You are how I was able to learn from my mistake!

"You mean cutting people up? The sacrifice was a mistake?"

Silly! Sometimes you are so funny. I can't stay mad at you, Ed. You are such a perfect disciple.

No, the sacrifices were perfection, given how I told them to do it. As I said, the mistake was mine. I didn't understand how human spirits worked. I thought that because the heart was the center of life, that removing the heart would bring life energy with it. Initially, I instructed them to remove the brains while the person was still alive, believing it would bring their knowledge with it.

But it didn't. Just like the hearts never brought enough life energy. Only the most negligible amounts. That's why we sacrificed so many. I tried old men, young men, old women, young women, children, babies. Millions of sacrifices, but we could never collect enough life, not in its truest essence.

But then, when I was searching for you, I discovered another old god. He was weak, weaker than me, so I ate him. When I did, I learned about the Chakras. It was so simple and so obvious.

"It sounds interesting, but I don't know what Chakras means."

I know, lovely one. No one knows. I am a knowledge eater! I keep most things for myself!

A person's life force, their true essence, it doesn't live in their hearts. The heart is where love and compassion come from. Worthless!

Baa!

Eating the hearts did so little and was so much work. We wasted so many magnificent bodies.

You have to eat the Muladhara! That's the good stuff. That's what I wanted you to see at Crystal River. I wanted you to see how to do it. And where to do it. We built that temple so long ago and sacrificed so many there, bringing them in by the boatload. There was so much energy! They were so terrified.

But now we need to do it correctly.

"What is the Muladhara?"

The voice told him.

Ed slammed on the car breaks, pulling over as quickly as he could, slamming the door open, and dry heaving just outside the car.

"Don't ever say that to me again!"

It's different for females.

She explained the difference.

"Stop it! Stop it!" Ed gagged again.

He sat there with his head in his hands. He believed he knew what the voice had intended but hadn't understood how it intended to accomplish its tasks. This was so much more gruesome than he had imagined.

That was the end of the conversation.

He sat at the roadside for a few hours. Frustrated that he could not talk to himself to process the information, instead, working ever so hard to keep negative thoughts out of his head.

After some time, he started the car back up. A day later, when he finally reached Dade County, he drove past the road to Florida City and ultimately arrived in Miami City midmorning on Wednesday. The land offices of Dade County were half an hour north of Miami City proper.

He entered the offices just as they were opening. Sheriff Stone's people had helped him get everything in order, initiating the title check. The land was owned by Dade County. It was part of a large block of parcels throughout the state that had not been purchased but had been cleared for sale. These parcels were valued at fifty dollars an acre, so the ten acres cost five hundred dollars.

The office confirmed Ed's wire from his bank, and Ed left three hours later with the notarized deed to the land in his briefcase.

He immediately drove to the Florida National Bank offices in downtown Miami City, signed in to his deposit box, and put the deed in the box next to its already near-full contents.

Out of curiosity, he drove to Turkey Point. There was no power plant there.

The power to Florida City is coming from somewhere. Where?

Ed drove to Homestead proper, the City of Homestead. They had power there from a new electrical plant they had built two years prior. The City of Homestead was only a few miles to the north of Florida City. This run of an electrical connection made much more sense.

They didn't want me to know it came from the City of Homestead because I might look into it and realize their fabrication about the county situation.

The electric power plant was very modern. It used a pulverized coal-fired boiler system. The coal was ground down into a fine powder. The idea was that the powder burned more thoroughly and more efficiently than coal bricks. The residue from the coal fell into a slag-trap, basically a large round receptacle half full of water. This was also sometimes called a wet-bottom-boiler.

From there, it was simple. The heat from the burning coal was used to boil water. The steam from the water turned turbines that generated power. The power was sent out of the plant in cables and distributed as usable electricity wherever the lines ran, and an interface was provided.

Ed was able to negotiate a tour of the facility, which took the rest of the day.

When finished, he ate in a diner close by, ultimately sleeping in his car again, parking it a few miles north, the direction farthest away from Florida City.

SMOKE LODGE

SOMETIME THAT WEEK

Stone thrashed about on the sandy floor of the small enclosed structure. The interior was lit by the large fire in its center. There were several ventilation holes in the top, a couple on different sides so the air could move between them, pulling enough new oxygen in and pushing enough carbon dioxide out to keep the fire burning.

The basic theory was that if there was enough good air for the fire to burn, there was enough good air to keep the occupants alive.

He wore nothing but a loincloth, the traditional Indian garb for a dream session, even though this was not a dream session. This was a cleansing, more of the body than the spirit. But in cleansing the body, the mind could become more focused. Cleansing visions were not as powerful as dream visions. However, the point was to get the chemicals out of his body, not introduce additional toxicity.

Stone was drenched in sweat.

The world came in and out of focus for him.

Every few hours, one of the three sisters would force him to drink more water.

He was aware of them; they wore the same traditional loincloth and nothing else. They would have to sometimes wrestle him and hold his head, forcing the liquid down. He was never sure, but it may have taken more than one of them from time to time. He knew he should be interested in these moments and in the sister's attractive symmetrical appearance.

But, in truth, he was too far gone to care.

Stone's exposed body showed major wounds and a history of violence.

There were whip marks on his back; his right shoulder had been shot through with a bullet multiple times, leaving significant scarring. There were knife cuts and healed puncture wounds up and down his front and back. One glance and his torso seemed to be the very definition of trauma.

Other than water, which he near immediately sweated away, he was given no food. The process was reasonably straightforward: purge the body of all toxins, introduce no new ones.

Where half a day or, in an extreme case, a full day in the lodge would have cleansed an ordinary man, by the time it was over, Stone was in for over three days, from late Monday night to early Friday morning. By the end, he dropped twenty pounds, his muscular form shedding the extra weight the sugar from the Coca-Cola had added over the years.

Since no hallucinogen had been used (or needed), Stone's session was what the Indians referred to as unguided. However, even an unguided session included a discussion at the end. Stone could consider what he saw and learned, and the medicine givers could reveal anything they learned about their patient or felt they needed to share.

As it stood, the session was near over; the fire had been allowed to die down to embers.

The sun would not be up for a few more hours, but Stone was coherent and sitting up. His body was exhausted, but his mind was clear. He sat cross-legged, a metal canteen close by with water that he drank from frequently. His dark hair was shiny and slicked back behind his ears, pulled into a knot. His skin sparkled and glistened in the low light, still wet from the process.

The three sisters sat across from him, Martha in the middle with Elizabeth and Alice on either side. Each woman stared intently at Stone, holding a look of anticipation and curiosity. The three sat silent; part of the ritual was to wait for Stone to be ready to discuss the experience.

He stared back at them, noticing slight differences between their otherwise identical appearances.

"I feel better." It was the first thought that occurred to him.

"You look better." Martha spoke for the three, it seemed. "When the sun comes up, we will cut your hair. Then we have water you can use to bathe and shave. We washed your clothes for you also. You will leave here a new man."

Stone smiled.

"Thank you," he said.

They sat in silence for a good while.

"I did not have any visions," Stone said finally.

Martha leaned forward. "We talked to several spirits during the time. One, Jack Abbott, has been trying to communicate with you. Another one, Maggie Summers, a powerful spirit, sensed you were in danger."

Stone, of course, knew about Jack Abbott and Maggie Summers. But Maggie was a surprise. Her story ended many years ago, and she transitioned to purgatory. A better outcome than she nearly experienced.

"How could you know about Maggie?"

Martha's face remained firm, holding eye contact. "She is a complicated one, Judge."

The embers popped, startling everyone.

Martha continued. "As she explained it, you saved her soul many years ago, fighting the shadows and risking your own spirit in the process. She explained that she knew all this but that for her, it had not happened yet. She was still on her initial journey, her spiritual walkabout, moving through space and time, exploring and visiting people and places."

Stone had not thought of that. He knew Maggie had a chance to move about between the time she died and the time he saved her soul. She told him as much. It just didn't occur to him what the implications of that might be.

"I would have liked the chance to talk to Maggie again," Stone said. It came out sounding introspective.

"I believe she has visited you many times, Judge. But she doesn't think it would be good for you two to talk again. Your business with her is done." Then Martha seemed to have an afterthought. "But, she is mighty fond of you, don't think otherwise. She impressed us, too, by the way. Explaining what you did for her. How you believed in her even given what she had done. How you could see the truth of it in its completeness.

"She presented the difference between God's law and man's justice, as you had explained it to her.

"We learned from her, Judge." Martha leaned

forward, her perfect youthful form glistening in the low light, shifting slightly with the movement. Her eyes bright, she continued. "It made so much evident to us. So many things we struggled to understand became clear." She leaned back, refocusing herself.

Everyone was quiet, then Martha continued.

"Judge, we're all believers. Elizabeth and Alice here. Myself, and Jorge. We're born again, each one of us. The biblical teachings align with our traditions and with our native gods. You just have to look before you, Judge. We believe. We do not see the conflict.

"Maggie, through your teachings, gave us the knowledge to know we have been right all along."

Stone nodded, allowing himself to remember Alamosa and Maggie for a bit, then pushing the thoughts away again. It all led down the same painful road. Anger replaced his sentiment.

Martha seemed to understand Stone's emotions. "Maggie leads to Jack. We all understand the relationship now." She nodded, indicating herself and her two sisters.

Stone's mood changed quickly. "I'm not ready to talk about Jack."

"It's been almost fifty years."

"I might be ready in another fifty; we'll see."

Stone started to stand.

"Wait." Martha reached over to keep him from getting up. "There was another spirit we talked to. The murdered boy, Eric Adams."

Stone sat back down. "I have already talked to him. He doesn't remember anything. I need to keep him with me so I can take him home and put him to rest."

The embers popped again. The dark room seemed to become darker.

"Judge, it is more complicated than you think. The boy suffered more than you know. The danger is significant."

"What danger?"

Somehow a breeze moved about the room. The temperature dropped; it became cold in the small confined space. The embers sparked and crackled like invisible water had been thrown on them, but instead of going out, they burned brighter.

"Judge, you work in a system. A spiritual system, but still one that relies on rules and boundaries. Your system is mainly Christian in its framing. Don't argue. I'm not saying biblical; I am saying Christian. Meaning you see things as good and evil, right and wrong. You see this life as a prerequisite to the next. You believe people have souls and that souls can be saved. Or not, that souls may suffer in an afterlife.

"That's a system. And it works, and it is mainly

correct, we three think. As I said, we believe.

"But we Indians see more, too. We know the world as a continuum. Everything is connected, the earth, the sky, the wind. Spirits exist inside us, then they return to the sky and the earth when we pass.

"The sky is vast; you call it the universe. We know there are ancestors out there as well. Some pure spirits, some more. There is a flow to things. Good follows good; evil follows evil.

"But the principles are the same. At their core, when you strip away the religion, the rules come down the same. Like Maggie told us. There is a truth in the foundation."

Martha watched Stone to make sure he understood.

He nodded that he did.

She continued. "But even our gods, and your god, they are young. Big, not small, for sure, but young compared to the beginnings.

"You see, at the beginning of the fifth age, the first gods, they were new, like us, for a while. But no longer. They are the old gods now.

"More primitive. More dangerous. More selfish.

"Their system is different. They started more literally. As an example, the Bible explains the Father, Son, and Holy Ghost. The Trinity. Three parts of the same thing. Inseparable. Perfection.

"The old gods, like the one that got Eric. They don't see the whole; they see the parts. They crave separation. They yearn for the best parts for themselves. They have no concept of redemption, or even value, to the whole. In their twisted pursuit of perfection, they want only the purest elements.

"The problem is, we're people. Humans. We're all blended together, the good and the bad. If you start pulling parts out, well, it doesn't go particularly well for us.

"Our gods, yours and mine, the new gods. They have people at their center. You could argue they are collectors, but that's a different argument. The foundation of it is that we, not them, are what's important. But, for the old gods and the ancient ones, they only care for themselves. They don't see us, only what we can give them. They chew us like steak and spit out the gristle."

Stone nodded. "So, what was done to the boy? He was separated? The old god taking the parts it wanted, discarding the rest?"

Martha composed herself. "Close, Judge. The parts she wanted, the old god, were eaten by her disciple. In this case, her proxy. But if she becomes stronger, she will have a physical presence here in this world. And her appetite is insatiable."

"His privates were eaten, right off him, while he was still alive and tied down. I know it because

I saw it. I know you speak the truth." Stone said while looking up at the small vents at the top of the tent.

"All that power and this old god is small right now, Judge. The smallest. Can you imagine what will happen if it grows in power? If it can collect the life energy it craves from more people? If it gains more believers?"

Stone, who a few moments ago believed he could imagine anything, realized that he could not have imagined this.

There was another long moment of silence. After several minutes the embers brightened, and the lodge became warm again.

"One more thing, Judge," Martha said. "I need to come with you to Miami City to put Eric to rest. In our conversations with him, he attached himself to me. I didn't choose it, but he did die a teenage boy, and I suspect following me around seems a lot more interesting than following an old beat-up cowboy around."

The spell was broken. Time stood still for several beats.

Stone wanted to argue but could feel Martha was right. He knew spirits did what they wanted, and he could not dispute Eric's logic.

Suddenly the world snapped back to how it was, the time and space of the small lodge returning to the time and space of the real world.

The conversation they had just had was now a thing of the past, no longer ever-present.

All at once, Stone realized he felt great and was sitting near-naked in a small hot room with three equally near-naked beautiful women.

Martha smiled at him as she and her sisters stood and worked their way out of the lodge.

"Well, there you go, Judge! It's good to have the old blood flowing again, I bet!"

***

Tap, tap. Scratch.

Rain.

Scratch.

Thunder. *Tap.*

Ed woke up. He had the windows closed to keep the rain out. It made the car warmer than he would have liked, but it was better than the alternative of letting water get in.

Lighting flashed off in the distance, thunder coming in five or six seconds later.

I must have slept through the start of the storm.

Generally, late-season Florida thunderstorms were much milder than the summer storms. The lightning tended to only be at the front of the storm, sometimes at the back too, but less often.

Scratch.

Ed heard the noise on the outside of the car. It sounded like a nail or tree branch rubbing against the vehicle on the passenger's side.

That's the side against the road; there aren't any trees or tree branches over there. What could be touching the car?

He turned his head this way and that to look out the windows around the car. He couldn't see anything between the darkness, the rain, and the light humidity fogging up the glass. He shifted in his seat and tried to go back to sleep.

Tap, tap. Scratch.

Ed sat straight up. That had been on his door. Whatever made the noise just a few inches from his head. He could hear something scratching that sounded like it was pushing hard enough to peel the paint.

BAM!

The car shook; it felt like something had jumped on and off the back bumper, hitting the rear trunk when it landed.

Ed screamed, his heart raced. Adrenaline and fear shot through his system.

He looked around but kept his head low, below the window line. He was breathing heavily, recovering from the shock. It was fogging the windows up even more.

Start the car and get out of here!

He quickly realized that he would need to go outside and turn the front starter crank to start the car.

What could be out there?

"Hello?" Ed yelled, not sure what else to do.

"Hello?" came back from outside. It was his voice with more primitive inflections.

Fear shot through him again. He realized he needed to go to the bathroom. He started to sweat, the interior of the car growing now very warm with his elevated metabolism.

SzeaSzhell, are you there? I need help!

A primal scream flooded in from outside, this time in front of the car. Whatever was out there was circling his vehicle and examining all sides.

SzeaSzhell, I need help!

Ed started to whimper, genuinely terrified.

Edward.

Not the loving statement. The voice was cold, like before on the drive back.

"SzeaSzhell! There is something outside!" Ed whispered loudly, his voice hoarse with dread.

The whole world is outside, Edward.

"Something jumped on the car and has been tapping and scratching the outside."

Edward, are you praying to me?

"What !?!" The question truly caught Ed off guard.

I need to know if you are praying to me. If you are, I can help. I am not so strong yet that I would turn away a true believer.

"I need help! It's trying to get me."

Edward, my worshippers, they ASK me for help. If you pray to me and ASK me for help, I will help you.

The thing outside screeched again and beat furiously on the back of the car for a few seconds, then stopped. The sound was unnerving and terrifying. The car shook with the force of it.

"SzeaSzhell, I am praying to you for help!" Ed whimpered, his head down with his arms over it, tucked as low as he could go in the front seat.

The wind gusted strongly outside, vibrating the car with its force.

There was a second screech off in the distance, followed by a loud close reply from something right outside Ed's door.

"SzeaSzhell?"

Oh, sorry, Ed. I'm busy. I have to relearn how to do two things at once. I spent so much time just talking to you that some of my skills have gotten rusty.

What did you need?

The thing started beating on the back of the

car again. Terrifying banging echoed in the small space. But it didn't stop like before; it kept battering the trunk. Suddenly, the car's front lurched down; something with substantial weight was pushing on the front bumper while the pounding of the car's back continued. Something cracked under a huge force.

"It's going to ruin the car and get me! IX-Chel, I pray to thee. Expel the intruder and save my life!"

Lightning flashed, and the storm intensified.

The outside clattering continued for a few seconds. Another lightning strike illuminated the sky. As the lightning flashed, Ed saw what looked like the face of an owl, a human owl woman, peering in the driver's window staring right at him, standing only inches away from the car.

Ed recoiled in fear. The thumping and commotion stopped. The owl-person was gone.

Everything seemed to be gone, the storm suddenly turned to a simple misty drizzle.

Was that a dream?

"SzeaSzhell?"

Ed waited a long time. He wasn't sure exactly how long, but it must have been an hour, if not two.

Nothing else happened.

Finally, the sky brightened. The rain was still

coming down, the first light of the new day making its way through the clouds from the east.

He looked outside the car through the still fogged up windows. From what he could see, everything looked normal. He could see the road and the bushes and the trees.

He waited longer, forcing himself to relax.

Finally, after another hour, when the light was good, after looking around as much as he could and not seeing anything, he cracked the driver's door open. When nothing bad happened, he opened the door entirely and stepped out.

The car was destroyed. All four tires were flat, the rear axle was cracked, and the rear was torn apart. The drive crank in the front was gone, the hood was smashed down, with the engine resting on the sandy ground underneath, covered in motor fluids that still dripped.

FUNERAL

NOVEMBER 22, 1919, 9 A.M.

The cold front had stalled over South Florida, raining nonstop now for two days. Everything was wet and cold, the temperature in the mid-fifties during the day and low forties at night. According to the *Miami Herald* meteorologist, the front should clear this morning at some point.

Stone and Martha stood off to the side. A primary group surrounded the outdoor casket as friends and family gave speeches about how great Eric Adams had been. It was a large service, a testament to Eric's standing in the local community.

Eric stood with Martha, staying close to her side. No one else could see him except Martha and Stone. The three listened intently to the service. Eric seemed unmoved, no longer invested in earthly accolades.

"Martha," he asked midway through, "I don't know who all these people are."

Martha Washington was dressed in a black skirt, the hemline just at her calves above the ankle. She wore a white and black blouse with an oversized collar that extended over her shoulders. The blouse had a very modest V-neck. She wore a black matching unbuttoned jacket and sensible black flats. Her long hair was pulled tight, tied into a bun.

Stone stood close to her, holding a men's umbrella over her to keep the rain off. The umbrella could close into a walking stick; it was a lovely piece, very modern-looking. Stone wore a sensible plain black suit with a white shirt and black tie. He looked a new man, clean, fit, and well-groomed. His hair was cut short, his salt-and-pepper beard neatly trimmed.

Both Stone and Martha wore slim black sunglasses. The pair had a look to them, Martha's symmetrical athletic beauty and Stone's rugged broad-shouldered frame. Where Stone looked solid and dangerous, Martha looked sleek and mysterious.

Without turning her head, Martha answered Eric in a soft voice. "Do you see your parents and family?"

"Yes."

"Your friends and school teachers?"

"Yes."

"Good. The rest are just well-wishers."

"I want to remember what happened. Everyone seems pretty shaken."

"You will remember in a few more moments when your body is placed into the ground."

Stone listened to the exchange, surprised with himself for feeling relieved that Martha was bearing the burden of dealing with the spirit. He had never in his life known another person who could do so.

Ed Leeds was standing farther away from the group. Not close enough to hear. It looked like he was staying his distance out of respect, waiting to talk to Stone once the event concluded. It made sense since he was not involved with Eric or the local community.

As the ceremony continued, the rain stopped. Stone retracted his umbrella. The clouds cleared, revealing Florida's classic bright blue November sky behind the cover. The sun's rays shown here and there, coming in through the sporadic clouds at the morning's angle.

It all made the cemetery a site to behold. Tall, aged oak trees, vibrant well-kept green grass, bright white tombstones, well-dressed mourners wearing their best black attire. Martha turned to Stone and smiled; he returned it. She turned to Eric and smiled at him; he returned it, looking vibrant and at peace.

As the last speaker stepped away from the podium, a shadow started to cross the sky, dimming the bright morning light. The darkness grew more pronounced. It was a lunar eclipse, the outline of the moon visible as it slowly worked its way across the round disk of the sun.

No one seemed to notice except Martha and Stone. The timing was working out that Eric's casket would be lowered as the moon reached its zenith. The feeling in the air changed, the calm, peaceful ambiance fading into a sense of tension. Martha reached down and took Stone's hand. Something was happening.

Without seeing him move, both Martha and Stone noticed Eric was now a few dozen feet away from them, approaching the casket and walking through the onlookers and attendees as if they were not there.

"Something's not right, Judge," Martha said, looking away from Eric and into Stone's eyes, then quickly back to Eric as he slowly walked forward. "We have to do something!"

Both Stone and Martha went to step forward, unsure how to intervene in the ceremony without causing a scene but knowing they must, both feeling the ominous sense of dread about what might be happening. However, neither could move. The eclipse was complete; the ceremony was in unnatural darkness.

Stone realized that it seemed as though time had stopped. He tried to speak to Martha but could not move. Everything was frozen in the last moment before Eric reached the casket, presumably approaching the light he would need to find to be saved.

Everyone was frozen in place. The wind had stopped. Only Eric moved, approaching the casket. Nothing happened; he looked confused. After a few moments, Eric turned back around, looking at Stone and Martha. But it was like he could not see them. Stone realized that since everything had stopped, it was possible Martha's light was not shining. Eric now seemed alone and lost in the darkness.

Suddenly Eric panicked. He cried for help, still looking back in Stone's direction. As though he could not move now either.

"Hello? Who's there?" Eric yelled as if in a dark room, worried he was not alone.

A strange-looking beast suddenly came into Stone's view. He tried to call out and warn Eric, but he could not; whatever had everyone else had him as well. The beast was short and wide, maybe four and a half feet tall. It moved through the crowd just as Eric had, oblivious to the other people, moving through them.

The creature was misshapen but not malformed. Its legs were short and its arms long, stretching from its narrow shoulders all the way to the ground. On its head were horns, like a moose or steer. Wide and heavy-looking. Its face was slightly elongated, not quite human-looking, not a snout like a dog or a wolf either. Its mouth was small for its frame.

Cold realization shot through Stone as he watched, helpless. The mouth looked like it matched the bite marks on Eric's body Stone had seen at the crime scene.

That would mean that this thing, or one just like it, was real.

The monster snapped its head around as if it heard Stone's thoughts. It made a motion of smelling the air, then its narrow eyes locked in on Stone. It moved towards him slowly, cautiously, stopping to sniff the air as it carefully came his way.

Stone wasn't one to get scared, not anymore. But frustration grew in him at his inability to move.

The creature advanced and came very close, maybe ten feet away. There it stopped, looking around, then changed its focus from Stone to Martha. It rubbed its exaggerated claw-laden hands together as if it had found a prize.

No, I'm the one who is awake, not her! Stone

screamed in his head.

The thing recoiled as though Stone had yelled at it, quickly refocusing on him instead of Martha for a moment. It started approached Stone again, looking at him intently, ready to react should Stone move.

When its face was inches from Stone's, it suddenly let out a bloodcurdling primal scream, looking directly at Stone and into his eyes. The creature's eyes were black empty circles; there was no life in them.

Stone could do nothing.

The creature screamed again, convincing itself that Stone could indeed not move, then refocusing on Martha.

If you touch her, I will end you.

The thing looked sideways at Stone when he thought those words. It no longer showed trepidation, quickly refocusing on Stone's beautiful companion.

Don't do it.

The thing stopped again at Stone's thoughts, but this time it used a mocking gesture, convinced it had all the power. It raised one of its hands to Stone's face and made a snipping motion, suggesting what it was about to do to Martha.

Then swiftly with no warning, it sprang, leaping onto her frozen form, swinging its razor-sharp claws this way and that, intent on disemboweling her.

But nothing happened. The monster could no more make contact with Martha than the other people in the crowd it had moved through. Stone relaxed the smallest amount when suddenly a powerful voice rang out from every direction.

"Bal-en-digo!"

It was a harsh, furious voice, like a master scolding their hound, full of anger and frustration at a dog that disobeyed in a critical situation.

The thing in front of Stone recoiled at the call, fear replacing its interest in Martha.

Eric called out again, clearly not able to see the goings-on. "Hello? Anyone? I can't move. I can't see anything!"

Balendigo, if that was the monster's name, turned its head slowly, hearing Eric's call, remembering its assigned task. Looking back to Stone and making the snipping motion again, savoring the display, it leaped into the air, bounding back around and directly at Eric, a renewed bounce in its step.

Stone tried to call out but to no avail.

Eric! he thought with all his might. If the monster could hear his thoughts, maybe Eric could as well.

Nothing.

The monster heard it, though, raising its hand and making a motion without turning around as it advanced towards Eric.

The darkness prevailed. Time was truly stopped as no eclipse lasted this long. Eric glowed in the dark, a beacon for the evil that stalked him.

When Balendigo was close, he leaped. Eric's scream filled Stone's head. Once down, Balendigo repeated the same wounds on Eric's spirit as had been inflicted on his physical body. The boy thrashed and pleaded and screamed in pain, crying for mercy. None was shown.

Since Stone could not turn his head or close his eyes, he watched the entire spiritual reenactment. He watched Eric suffer, eaten alive by the misshapen monstrosity. It took some time, the monster working carefully so as not to extinguish Eric until it was unavoidable. The irony of the frozen funeral bystanders ripe against the horrific show, Eric already at his gravesite but now cursed to never find eternal peace.

When it was over, Stone expected the eclipse to end. Time remained frozen for so long Stone grew worried. Eventually, another figure appeared, coming into view lazily in the dark day.

If Balendigo was terrifying, this new figure was petrifying. It radiated such power and danger that there was no avoiding a moment of pause, the rational mind not able to comprehend initially what it was witnessing. The new figure stood at least seven feet tall; it had the face of an owl but with a human woman's features. It was pure white, white feathers on the white wings and body. Both its hands and feet were long, with sharp talons.

The owl woman walked to Balendigo and put its hand on him. It reminded Stone of a person with their trusted dog. Balendigo responded to the touch, seemingly proud of the recognition. After the moment ended, Balendigo looked over to Stone. The owl creature followed his gaze.

Stone felt fear for the first time in a great while, for the first time he could remember since Alamosa several decades ago. He tried to move again but could not.

As the owl thing floated his way, his fear grew.

Get a hold of yourself, man.

"Yes." The voice was pleasant, loving, and kind-sounding. "Calm down. There is no need to fear me."

Stone watched it approach. It paused a few feet away from him, then sensing something, stopped. Not advancing close like Balendigo had.

"You are an interesting one!" Its head tilted from side to side, taking Stone in. "You have been touched by the new gods, haven't you!" She moved closer after her realization.

Stone's fear was gone, replaced with anger.

I didn't recognize you before. But now I see you, Stone thought. *You hide it well, but you are just a shadow, just like the others I have dealt with. You feed off the little sins; I know you. The moments between the moments, like now.*

"What is your name? Mine is, to your ear, SzeaSzhell. IX-Chel to my worshippers!"

Names have power, old one. You may know me as the shadow eater.

"Digugodisgi!" she said after a moment. It was Stone's spirit name: Judge.

You are not powerful. I can feel your weakness. You are only able to exhibit power now in your realm. Yes, you have a few believers. Yes, you can summon charlatan tricks and do small phenomena in the real world in their presence. But it costs you. Who is your believer here, I wonder?

Stone could sense that there was building power, though. This shadow thing was currently small, but it was an old god, and it could grow to be very dangerous.

The owl spirit moved close, reaching her taloned hand into Stone, cupping his heart. He felt the iciness of it and his fear, in part, returned.

"Mortal! But not like the others. You have been touched, as I said. You have a purpose, but there is no glory in it. You work hard for little, offering no salvation, only transition. What woe you sow! What a glorious curse!"

It was all true; the thing was able to understand Stone's contract. The trade he had made that no heaven-bound soul had ever made before, even though it was offered to every single one.

Stone grew very angry.

Why did you do that to the boy's spirit? What gain is there for you? You already took his life!

The owl thing removed its hand from Stone's heart, stepping back a few feet and spreading its wings wide.

"I am hungry!" It flapped its wings, making a show of it. "Waste not, want not! Doesn't your god tell you that? Eat of the body and eat of the spirit!"

IX-Chel flapped her wings, rising off the ground. Stone could feel no wind from it

The ground began to vibrate, tiny rays of light cracking the darkness from the edges of the eclipse, through the sky, and into the cemetery.

"I cannot hold this moment any longer, Digugodisgi. But I know of you now. Balendigo has told me of your beautiful friend too. Her spirit is so bright like yours used to be before your journey started.

"I have glory ahead; you nothing but woe and strife. I can barely contain the anticipation!"

***

Ed parked his brand new 1919 Pierce-Arrow Model 31 on the paved road at the edge of the Miami City Cemetery. The car was the most expensive hardtop he could find. He paid over eight thousand dollars for it, buying it and driving it off the dealer lot in Palm Beach yesterday. It was a magnificent machine. Painted a dark blue with black trim and white tires.

The Model 31 was designed as a limousine. It had an enclosed front seat with a window behind it, separating the driver from the passengers. The back was pure luxury, with two sitting chairs and two bench seats. Ed slept in it last night and had the best sleep of his life, able to stretch out his five-foot frame for maximum comfort.

He parked last night in downtown Miami City, not willing to risk nighttime isolation for fear of whatever it was that had attacked him earlier.

The service for Eric Adams was already underway when he arrived. Possibly, a hundred people gathered near the gravesite. He saw the Citrus County sheriff standing back from the main group. A woman stood with him; they made an attractive couple. The sheriff looked healthier than just a few days ago when Ed had talked to him before. His hair was washed and cut; he looked to have lost some weight. How he did it in the five or so days since Ed had last seen him would be an interesting conversation starter.

Ed waited for the ceremony to end. The sky cleared, and the rain stopped. As the casket was lowered into the ground, there was a flash of sunlight. Ed watched the people gathered to offer their condolences to Eric's parents, then slowly made their way away.

When he looked back, Sheriff Stone was leaning on the woman he was with, his arm stretched out for support with his head down. The two were talking feverishly; their mood seemed to have changed quickly from calm to agitation. He waited longer for everything to clear out, then walked up to Stone, waving as he approached, making sure Stone saw him before he was too close.

"Hello, Sheriff," Ed said when he was within earshot.

The sheriff acknowledged Ed with a wave, righting himself and standing tall.

"Hello, Mr. Leeds." He motioned with his hand for Ed to come closer. "Mr. Leeds, I would like to introduce"—the sheriff paused and looked at the woman for a second, both exchanging a glance that Ed did not understand.—"my wife, Martha."

The woman made a face of confusion but quickly recovered, turning to Ed with her hand out, palm down. "Hello, Mr. Leeds; it is a pleasure to meet you."

Ed accepted her hand very briefly, then released it. The woman was stunningly attractive. She was an Indian, her striking blue eyes softening her native features. Ed found that it was hard to look at her for too long least he discovered he could not pull his gaze away.

"I would not have guessed you were the marrying type, Sheriff," Ed said conversationally.

The sheriff smiled back but looked very shaken otherwise. "Recent events warrant surprising concessions, Mr. Leeds."

Ed smiled at the statement. *I have no idea what that means,* he thought to himself as he held his smile for what he hoped was a correct social duration.

"Sheriff, are you okay? You are white as a ghost," Ed noticed and asked before he could think the question through.

Stone nodded to him a couple times. "I actually just had a spell, Mr. Leeds. Thank you for asking. I am not familiar with Miami City. Do you know a place we three could sit down and discuss events? We have much to talk about."

Ed nodded. "Yes, there is a diner near here that I used to eat at all the time when I was selling air conditioners. It is only a few minutes by car. Please follow me. I am happy to drive us."

RASCAL HOUSE DINER

NOVEMBER 22, 1919, LUNCH TIME

Ed kept a close eye on the tab. Martha had two eggs, bacon, toast, and coffee, which was six-five cents. Sheriff Stone ordered the same thing but with an extra orange juice, which was an additional ten cents, so seventy-five cents for him. Ed didn't eat much; he ordered from the ala carte menu: toast, coffee, and marmalade for a total of twenty-five cents.

The check would be one-dollar sixty-five cents. Then there was the gratuity. Ed knew what to watch for; people would often try and cheat him and divide the gratuity three ways on the total. Trying to get him to pay a third of the eighteen cents additional fee, six cents, instead of just the amount on his part of it, two cents.

They ate with little conversation; Ed distracted, keeping an eye out for the bill so he could get a jump on making sure it was divvied up correctly. When they were done, and the waitress brought the check, Ed tried to reach for it, but the sheriff got it first.

Here we go, Ed thought. *He better not try and get me to cover the whole thing; that's also a tried and true trick. Hey, thanks for showing us around your city! How about picking up the tab!*

Instead, to Ed's amazement, the sheriff handed the waitress two dollars without even recalculating the amounts and making sure they didn't try and slip something in that no one ordered. That was a ploy he watched for too.

"Keep the change," Stone said with a polite smile.

Keep the change? Thirty-five cents on a dollar-sixty-five tab? That's outrageous. That's breakfast tomorrow he just gave away today! No wonder no one has a savings account here in this country.

Ed's internal dialogue often went like this when not fighting to save the world from ancient old gods hell-bent on torture-killing everyone ever born and eating their soul.

Martha looked at Ed and put her hand on his. "Ed, thank you for driving us here and for recommending this diner. You were right; the food was excellent." She squeezed his hand and then let it go.

Ed turned bright red, taken by surprise at the show of gratitude and familiarity. He was also in the afterglow of a free meal, a big deal for him.

I suppose I shouldn't try and get them to pitch in for the gas that got us here, given they paid for breakfast. Should I? No, if I count the cost of breakfast, they have a couple gallons on account with me.

His plan had been to bring up the gas cost as the check was being divided. His salesman's brain knew it was easier to get money from someone when their wallet was already open.

The waitress refilled everyone's coffee cup. You got free refills here which was the main reason Ed liked the place.

Finally, the sheriff started the business conversation; Ed had been dreading it. The voice did seem to be off doing something else. Sheriff Stone apparently drove it away; it was also absent the last time he sat with Stone at the start of this terrible week.

"Mr. Leeds," Stone said, looking directly at him, "there has been some development. The good news is that you are cleared of any interest in Eric Adam's case. We now know that the events surrounding his death were, well, unusual."

Ed was relieved, but also a spark of curiosity lit

in him.

How could he know things were unusual? The Indian woman seems to know something also. I wonder if I can trust them?

Ed put his salesman persona on. "At the risk of enrolling myself when you have just cleared me, Sheriff, what do you mean unusual? I know the murder was gruesome; is that what you mean?" Ed spoke with as much charisma as he had, which was considerable when he was selling.

Stone looked at Ed for a moment. It struck Ed as an odd way of looking at him, not looking directly at him but more looking around him, like he was trying to see how much Ed glowed or something.

The diner was bright; they sat in a window booth looking out at Brickell Avenue. Brickell was a main road with business on the west side and the beach and ocean on the east side. It was too cold today for the beaches to be full of people, so instead, the view was the pretty white sand and slowly rolling ocean waves moving in and out from the Atlantic.

Sheriff Stone seemed to make a decision. "It was supernatural."

Martha looked at Stone and gave a slight nod like she agreed to use that term and to tell Ed.

Ed was both shocked, scared, and excited by the sheriff's comment.

"Supernatural?" he blurted out before he could get in front of his own thoughts or polish his response.

"You seem almost relieved, not surprised," Martha said.

Ed turned red again. "Well, er, I mean, what else could it be, right? The Indian pyramid and gruesome scene."

"That mound is not Indian. It was used by the Mayans, but it is even older than them. We call the builders the rubber people. The before people."

Ed leaned back in the booth. He sat on one side of the table, Martha and Stone on the other side, with Martha closest to the window.

"I read about the Maya, about how they had a huge empire and used to make sacrifices. Terrible stuff. Scary. But I have never heard of rubber people."

Stone interrupted. "Mr. Leeds, why were you reading about ancient Mayan history?"

"Please call me Ed. Everyone calls me Ed. I told you the other day. I am looking to support university research." It was a lie but a convenient one. "Can I tell you something? It will sound crazy, but you brought it up, not me."

The Indian woman knows something. She will know how to help, Ed decided.

"Of course," Stone said.

The traffic on the street outside, both the road and people walking, had picked up. The storm front passed just as the newspaper said it would, but it was still very breezy, making the already cold day seem all the colder.

Ed turned his attention to Martha. "In Indian history, have you ever heard of someone called IX-Chel?" He made sure to use the proper inflections.

Martha looked at Stone again; he nodded to her. Then she said, "Yes, Ed. In Mayan history, not Indian, that is the name of a goddess. She was the god of the moon and fertility."

Ed was surprised. "That doesn't sound too scary?" It came out as a question.

Martha smiled. "Well, we women can be a little scary"—she smiled—"but no, she is not a particularly scary deity."

"Did people used to make human sacrifices to her?"

Martha looked back at him in surprise. "No, not that I am aware of. Her job was to make sure the moon moved as it was supposed to and that babies were conceived. She also helped with the rain since rain is life, babies need water to grow up strong, and people need water to live so they can procreate."

"Are you sure? That doesn't sound right."

"Yes, Ed, I am sure."

Ed thought for a few moments.

"What would a scary Mayan god have been?"

Maybe this voice has been lying to me about who it is. It has lied so many times; I shouldn't have just believed it when it told me its name.

Martha thought, reaching over and putting her hand on the sheriff's hand, which seemed to surprise him.

They sure don't seem to know each other like a married couple would.

"Well, Ed," Martha returned, "a really scary old Mayan god, the first one that comes to mind is Yum-Kimil. Yum-Kimil is sometimes a man and sometimes a woman. It is often said she has the parts of both a man and a woman. She is the god of death and reigns dominion in hell."

That sounds more like it, Ed thought.

"That sounds more like it," Ed said at the same time he thought it.

"Sounds more like what?" Sheriff Stone said, studying Ed.

Uh-oh. I have to start thinking before I speak! Oh well, I am going to tell them. If they can't help, no one can.

Ed leaned forward. "I didn't tell you, Sheriff, because it sounds crazy. I only barely believe it myself, but some things have happened this week since we last spoke that have forced me to come to terms with the reality of the situation."

"Go on."

"I seem to be haunted by a voice that claims to be IX-Chel. She speaks to me in my head. She told me to go to Crystal River. She wanted to show me something.

"I thought at first that the voice was just in my head or that someone like a magician or mystic was projecting it there. But then, on the way back a couple days ago, I saw something terrifying. More than saw it, it attacked me. Well, I was in my car; it destroyed my car."

Ed made a *Can you believe it?* face, still looking primarily at Martha.

"What did the thing look like?" Martha asked.

They're not going to believe me, but I think this is my only chance for help.

"There were two of them. The one that attacked me looked like, well, it's hard to describe. It looked like a human dog with antlers. The scary one, the one I think is the voice, which I only saw for a few seconds as lightning flashed, looked like a giant owl person."

"Where was this attack?" Stone jumped in, energetic.

"It was a couple miles north of the Homestead downtown."

"I would like to see the car."

"That's fine, I can take you. I had to walk back and leave it."

Stone started to get up, Ed spoke quickly.

"Wait, Sheriff, there is more. The voice—that's what I call it—told me that it had found new believers. This is very dangerous. It seems to get power and strength from having people believe in it."

Stone settled back down, making a motion to the waitress for a coffee refill. When she left the table, he asked, "Do you know who these new believers might be?"

"Yes, actually I do. The voice used a term that I think identifies them. She said that these new believers were part of a flock with a pastor and already had a house of worship. She called it a cathedral."

"How is that helpful?"

Ed smiled a very weak smile. "Because these are the same people that are in Florida City, some of which, anyway, are trying to cheat me by pretending to be able to sell me the land I wanted. The pastor there is Pastor Rick Weller. When I spoke with him the other night, he used the word cathedral very prominently. And, if he is in on the land scam, he doesn't have strong Christian values, which means he may not be a true believer."

Stone leaned back. "I had forgotten about the land. Were the Citrus County people helpful?"

"Oh yes, thank you. I had almost forgotten too. They were very accommodating. I purchased the land and have the deed. It was the simplest transaction, right at the Dade County office. It only took a couple hours."

Stone nodded. "Have you confronted the Florida City people?"

Ed shook his head no. "Not yet. I don't really want to, but since the city is close to my new property, well, I guess there is no way around it."

Stone looked at Martha for a few moments, then back to Ed. Stone's eyes were bright and mischievous when he looked back. "Ed, part of my job is to keep things in balance. It's a complicated job, and it isn't always clear what the right thing to do is, or even when things become unbalanced. However, it is clear to me that this voice of yours needs to be stopped.

"I will ease your mind. I saw the same two creatures you did. I saw them at the funeral. They could not interact with the physical world there, but they were complex shadows, so I have no doubt that they can interact as their energy grows.

"They were just as you described. After talking to Martha, we both think these are somehow old gods trying to reinvigorate themselves. But make no mistake, this is evil we are dealing with. I saw what they did to Eric's spirit, same as his body. No good can come from them."

Ed was ecstatic.

I can't believe I am going to get some help!

"How can we fight them?" he asked.

Stone shook his head and looked at Martha. "I don't know. I have fought many shadows, which is what we are dealing with here when it is all boiled down. But, even with the powerful ones, I always had a spirit attachment. My job, each time, was to help the spirit find peace in the physical world so they would be strong enough to confront the shadows in their spirit world.

"I would help the spirit understand themselves and to learn how the laws of the spirit realm work, which brought them power. But I don't have that here without an attachment."

Ed noticed that Martha was staring at Stone intently. It seemed she knew some of this, but not all of it.

Ed finally had to ask. "Are you two really married?"

Stone answered, "Let's say we are undercover. I think the two of us are easier to explain as a married couple than as a sheriff outside of his jurisdiction with his Indian deputy's sister medicine woman in tow."

Ed thought for a few minutes. Stone was right.

It was a lot easier to accept them when introduced as a married couple. "I see your point," he returned, finishing his third coffee, feeling pretty good as the caffeine finally kicked in.

THE SMASHED CAR

NOVEMBER 22, 1919, 2 P.M.

The day remained cold and windy. The drive out was uneventful. Ed drove his new car; Stone and Martha both rode in the front with him, with Martha in the middle. They moved along a white sand and dirt road with palmetto bushes and weeds on either side. The road itself was primarily one lane, although there was just enough room for two cars to pass each other if both drivers were slow and careful.

As they approached Ed's car, Stone studied it. Ed had said it was beaten to the point of being unrepairable, which certainly seemed the case in its appearance. Stone was interested in the physical damage and anywhere that the spirits had touched the vehicle.

A growing sense of dread filled him when he saw the violent impacts. The sheer power on display was staggering. He might have been wrong in his assessment that these spirits were just more specific versions of the shadows he had faced before. The shadows were powerful entities, but they could do nothing like this on their best day. If it had been explained correctly, IX-Chel, or whatever the thing called itself, was without a worshipper base. The thought that it was actively trying to grow in strength was suddenly terrifying.

No wonder it so freely offered me the name IX-Chel. It is hiding behind that name; that's not its real name. Otherwise, why give it up so quickly? Why offer me power over it so easily?

Stone was caught up in his own thoughts. He was still upset about what he had seen at the funeral and what happened to Eric's spirit.

I shrugged my responsibilities, and Eric's eternal soul is in hell because of it. I shouldn't have let Eric attach himself to Martha. She did everything she could, but it was my duty, and I failed him. When the immediacy of this situation is over, I will fix it, even if I have to go to hell myself and bring him back.

Ed parked. Stone got out and walked around the smashed car, carefully looking at the different dents and scratches, using his sheriff's eyes. He also looked in the soft white sand and dirt around the car. He could see Ed's footprints, where he got out of the driver's door, stood, then started the long trek back to civilization. There were two other sets of prints.

Not that I needed independent confirmation, I believed Ed, and the car is smashed to pieces, but I can see the two prints from the shadows in the ground. They were real and whole in this world.

He bent down and examined a couple sets of marks on the ground. One was more prominent, seemingly moving slower, the prints more pronounced.

"Martha, can you come over here and look at this, please?" Stone called to her. She and Ed had stayed away initially so Stone could have a complete run of the scene.

Martha walked over.

"Do you see here and here?" Stone indicated at points where there were deep indentations on the edges of the footprints. "This thing has four talons. Sometimes three in front and one in back. Sometimes two and two." Then, pointing to the side of the car where there were matching scratches in the paint, he added, "But see here, it is always three when attacking."

Martha looked at the differences. "Owls can do that. They have an opposable claw that they can rotate."

"The shadows I deal with, when they try and attack the living, they always leave their marks like this on the car. In sets of three. It is a sign of identification as much as a wound, meant to mark a victim so other shadows can follow them and help finish the job"

Martha walked over to a clear piece of ground away from the car and motioned for Stone to follow. She drew an arc in the dirt with two lines through it. "Look for this marking also. It is the sign of separation. It means that the victim has no value, that they are not a complete soul. I have seen spirits leave this mark as well, but I do not see it here."

Stone stood up and looked back at the car from a few feet away. "These things are powerful, Martha. More powerful than what I often deal with. Usually, I have an attachment that is trying to figure things out, like I said, and my job is to give them the tools to understand themselves. I have no idea how to fight a giant Mayan owl god and its minions. I don't know what tools to use."

Martha looked back at him, still wearing her dark sunglasses. "I think the foundation is the same. Seek the truth, do what's right. Also, and I hesitate to point this out, you do have a spirit attached to you. You have Jack Abbott."

Stone frowned. "I'm not bringing him into this. Martha, that's more complicated than you know. I owe Jack a debt, but I haven't figured out how to repay it yet."

Martha nodded. "Well. I can summon my

ancestors; I can summon yours too. I know the rituals."

He frowned at her. "I fear they would be lost, eaten by this thing before we figured out how to defeat it."

The wind picked up. The two stood in the cold sunlight for several minutes, looking at the car and thinking. The wind blew, reassuring Stone that time had not stopped. Stone's gaze shifted from the mangled vehicle to Martha and her strong silhouette as they stood. His thoughts were slowly going from the immediate danger on display to the long-term possibility of a partner in his difficult struggles against the shadows.

It seemed, after a moment, she felt his gaze, turning to look at him sideways. They locked eyes and seemed to have an ease with each other that neither had felt before. This was the beginning of a bond forming right here, at this moment.

She reached over and took his hand, the warmth between people against the cold and windy day. Stone could see her bright blue eyes behind the dark glasses. They had a spark in them and an unsaid desire that he had not noticed before.

After a few more minutes, the spell was broken when Ed called over to them.

"That was interesting," Martha said, coming back down to the here and now.

"It seems we may have some serious discussions in front of us," Stone returned, surprised. "Come on over, Ed!" He yelled so Ed could clearly hear him.

In a low voice, Martha said to Stone with a seductive smile, "Discussions? We Indians have some other words for it."

Ed walked over. "I thought maybe you two were frozen."

Stone returned to the subject at hand. "Ed, what else can you think of about these shadows? We can see they are powerful. We need to figure out how to stop them before they become too powerful."

"The only thing I know is what I already told you. The voice constantly talked about getting more believers and how more believers would restore some of her power. I have had the voice in my head for nearly ten years, Sheriff. I never thought it was real like this. And it never did anything to suggest it was. It would yammer on from time to time, confusing me at important moments. But I never told anyone about it, and nothing physical like this ever happened until a few nights ago."

"Not until it told you it had found more believers," Martha said.

"Exactly," Ed returned.

Stone stepped forward and turned so he could

talk to both Martha and Ed while looking them straight on. "Ed. Let's run your land acquisition to ground."

"I already told you, I got the deed. I own the land."

"Hold on, let me finish. Let's go back to Florida City and go along with this mayor and the whole scheme. We can use it to get close to Pastor Rick, see what that's about. If it turns out that they have turned from a church to a cult, we'll deal with it."

"So," Martha said, "instead of trying to fight the spirits directly, we will instead remove their power base?"

"Right. I can't arrest the scammers, though. I'm not the sheriff around here."

"Wouldn't matter if you did, Sheriff." Ed looked sad. "If they have seen what IX-Chel can do, they will believe for as long as they live."

Everyone was silent.

Finally, Stone spoke. "It's going to be hard killing women and children. But I have done it before."

"There must be another way!" Martha said earnestly, not wanting to think about Stone's implications.

He looked at her. *I haven't had a partner in the supernatural component of this before. I never had resources beyond my own. I need to start thinking in terms of what I can do and what an Indian medicine woman can do to help.*

"You're right, Martha. I have only had one toolset up until now. We might still need to do it my way, but I don't want to do it any more than you do. Do you have some idea or suggestion on another way to go about this?"

She smiled. "The seesaw is a lot more fun with someone to balance on it with you, Judge."

"That it is. What is your suggestion?"

"Well…" She looked at the ground, thinking. "What if they don't remember what they saw? What if we could get them all to forget?"

Stone frowned. That didn't sound plausible.

Ed's face lit up. "I got it!"

Both Stone and Martha turned to look at him.

"What if they stop believing?"

Stone let his face show irritation. "You just said two minutes ago that once they see what IX-Chel can do, they will believe for the rest of their lives!"

"I did, and it's true. But then I remembered something. I saw a man last year in Atlanta. Harry Houdini. Have you ever heard of him?"

Neither Stone nor Martha had.

"He is famous in the north and around the world, I think. He is an illusionist. I saw his show and, for weeks afterward, believed that he had genuine magic powers. I guess I still do believe it at some level. What he was able to do was amazing! The police were there; they put him in chains just like he was the worst kind of criminal. Then in seconds, he was out of the chains! And they checked him first; he didn't have a key or anything.

"And no, before you ask, the police were not in on it. Just the opposite. They were greatly embarrassed that he got free. Their pride was shattered."

"So?" Stone said.

"So, it introduced doubt into my beliefs. I will truly doubt forever that shackling can hold a man. It doesn't mean it can't, just that I will never forget what I saw firsthand."

"So?" Stone said again.

"So maybe we can just introduce doubt somehow. Convince Pastor Rick and his congregation that what they believe they saw was a trick. Introduce doubt. It might not work with everyone, so more, um, severer measures might be necessary. But it will work on children for sure, and it's a better plan than just killing everyone!"

"It allows for hope, Judge," Martha said as the wind continued to blow in the cold afternoon.

"I'm willing to try it. Martha, I have an idea of what we need. We can discuss it tonight when we have some time alone. Ed, are there rooms somewhere in Florida City?"

"Yes, they have a flophouse, and the Palm Street Tavern has some nice rooms upstairs. But they are a dollar a night. I mean, I know the owner, so maybe we can negotiate that."

"A dollar a night is fine," Stone said, not completely oblivious to the benefits of a private room and some time alone with Martha.

Ed snorted. "Must be nice to be made of money, Sheriff!"

FLORIDA CITY

NOVEMBER 22, 1919, 4 P.M.

Coral came running out of the Palm Street Tavern as soon as Ed got out of the car. She did a double take when she realized it was a different car altogether from the one he usually drove.

"Ed!" she yelled as she ran to embrace him.

Ed was his usual uncomfortable self with the public show of affection. He never understood why Coral was so interested in him or what signals he was sending to suggest he was open to her advances.

Not that I am not, of course. But I still can't figure it out.

As she embraced him, she whispered in his ear, "Ed! I have a lot I need to tell you! Be careful with this lot here; everything is not as it seems! Let's talk privately as soon as we can."

Then standing away so her voice could be heard

broadly, she said, "Ed, it's great to see you! Mayor Laundry's kids have gone missing! Can you believe it? Who are your new friends? Where did you get the new car?"

A rush of energy and questions.

Ed tried to recover. "Coral, this is Mr. and Mrs. Sher—"

Stone jumped in. "My first name is Isaac, ma'am. This is my wife, Martha." He reached over to shake Coral's hand.

Coral didn't miss a beat, shaking Stone's hand vigorously and smiling. "It's wonderful to meet you! How do you know Ed?"

"We're friends of Ed's from Tampa. I help the state college with historical excavation work." This was technically true. "Ed has been gracious enough to offer to help support the history department. Martha and I were just in the area and ran into him. He insisted we come out here and see this piece of land he is so excited about."

"Donors? Do you mean money? Ed, I had no idea you could afford to donate money to a university! How exciting!"

Ed started to explain something, but a look from Stone cut him off again. He instead smiled a thin smile to suggest his agreement.

"Ma'am," Stone said, "did I understand you to say some children went missing?"

"Oh yes, Mr. Stone."

"Please, use my common name. Judge."

"Okay, *Judge.*" Coral smiled and curtsied like she was addressing royalty, making a funny face at Ed when she did it. "Mayor Laundry has two daughters, Lara and Betty. For the past week, he thought they were with Mrs. Laundry back in Miami City. See, he and the missus prefer to live separately, and the girls only come out to Florida City a couple of times a month to see him.

"Apparently, in the middle of last week, they talked their mother into staying here longer since they couldn't come out next week because of the upcoming Thanksgiving holiday, so she left without them. But Gary—that's the mayor's first name—says that the girls didn't check with him and that he didn't know they stayed. It wasn't until this afternoon when their mom came to pick them up again that the whole mess came to light."

Missing children in the middle of this IX-Chel fiasco could be terrible news. I don't know if I have it in me to find another body in the same condition as Eric Adams, Stone thought to himself.

Not knowing what else to say, Stone said, "Are they starting to look for them? We would be happy to help."

Coral nodded. "Yes, everyone is inside. Come on, follow me!"

She looked at Ed and made a serious-minded face at him, reminding him what she had whispered several moments ago.

The inside of the tavern was lit with the new electric lamps. They gave off a weird yellow light, and there was just the slightest of hums in the background. Still, none of the kerosene oil smell lingered in the room from the old oil lamps, so it was a trade-off in which sense was assaulted.

There were eight people in the tavern, talking loudly. Mayor Gary Laundry was in the center of the small group, his face red. He was some combination of hugely depressed, manic to get going and find his girls, and fearful at the edges that it has been too long and their fates may already be sealed.

Standing next to Laundry were two church pastors. Pastor Rick Weller, who Ed suspected of being the new believer in the voice, and Pastor Carry Sanders, the head of the colored church. Pastor Rick and his congregation were Presbyterians; Pastor Carry and her congregation were Baptist. They actually got along very well; they shared an inside joke between them: for every fourth follower either pastor found, the other would bring a fifth to celebrate.

Bahama Bill, the owner of the tavern, was there behind the bar. He placed the old lamps that had been replaced by the electrical lights on the bar and were working to fill each one with oil. Every now and then, he would go into a door behind the bar that led to the small apartment where he and Coral lived, returning with a piece or part.

Sally Jones was there in the small circle, also listening and nodding. Her two boys, Billy and Ron, were with her. Jill Hayes, an older teen who worked for Sally making pastries, was the last person in the group.

"Ed's here! He has two friends with him that can help in the search!" Coral announced as she energetically walked Ed, Stone, and Martha into the room.

When Laundry saw Ed, he tried to show appreciation, but it came across as forced given his concern for his family.

"Ed," Laundry said, "I got the announcement to run in the paper just like we discussed. We should be all set for the auction!"

Pastor Rick put his hand on Laundry to reassure him, then turned to Ed, sensing the awkwardness. "Gary is continually working to help others!" Then, to Gary, he said, "Mayor, now is not the time to worry about land. We need to find Betty and Lara."

Laundry nodded; his energy was coming in waves, a balance between genuine exhaustion and frantic concern.

Stone, Ed, and Martha exchanged knowing glances but could not talk amongst themselves because of all the people in the small space. Everyone in the room introduced themselves, as did Stone and Martha.

If I had to, I would think that this Pastor Rick fellow is in on the land scam, Stone thought. Then, as was his nature, he addressed the room.

"Everyone," he spoke loudly, knowing that as a perceived outsider, some may not want to hear from him, but slipping into his role as always, and addressing his consistent need to try and help others, a need he carried almost like an addiction.

I could use a Coca-Cola, and a shot of whiskey flashed through his mind, but he continued anyway. "I served as a major in the war." They would assume the Great War, not the Civil War. "One of the units I ran was a rescue unit. If you like, Mr. Laundry, I can help you get organized and maximize the efficiency of your search."

Laundry looked surprised and unsure. Pastor Rick stepped in again to speak for him. "I think that would be terrific, Mister...?"

"Stone," Stone finished for him. "But I prefer to go by Judge. No mister, just Judge."

"Well, Judge," Pastor Rick said, trying the name out, "we would welcome the help. We have been working amongst ourselves, trying to come up with the best approach. It is going to be dark in ninety minutes or so."

Stone stepped forward, all business. Laundry may be the head of the grift to steal money from Ed, but his two children weren't. Stone could put the father's discretions aside long enough to try and help the children. "The girls have been missing for how long?"

"A week and a half!" Laundry blurted, clearly shaken, sobbing behind the statement.

"Okay. That's a long time." Stone softened his voice; Laundry was clearly genuinely upset. "I need to ask some difficult questions. These questions are for everyone. Mr. Laundry, is that okay with you?"

Laundry nodded, looking anxious.

"Do we know for a fact that the girls were here in town before they disappeared? Oh, and how old are they?"

"Betty is fifteen, Lara is twelve," Laundry returned. "Yes, I visited with them late last week, before their mother was supposed to pick them up. They were here alright."

Stone thought quickly. "Okay, fifteen is a very mature age. That could help us. Is it possible they wandered off and got lost?"

Pastor Rick answered. "We just got done discussing that before you got here. The girls have been coming here for a couple of years. They know the area well. We don't think they could have gotten lost. Now that's not the whole story. I mean, there are dangerous animals out there—rattlesnakes, alligators, panthers..."

Laundry made a whimpering sound; Pastor Rick looked at him, then back to Stone.

"Sorry, Gary. But Judge, sir, you get the idea."

Stone nodded, then looked at Billy and Ron Jones. "Gentlemen"—he nodded to their mother Sally—"would you two please go outside and scan the horizon for both smoke and for vultures circling in the sky?"

Laundry made the whimpering sound again.

Sally nodded her understanding, gently pushing the two boys toward the door. "Go on now. Don't go off the front walkway, but do as the man says. As soon as you see something, come back in here and tell us."

The two boys hurried out, trying to decide if they had just been dismissed and they would miss the important adult talk or if instead they had just been given a key assignment and they were somehow now a vital part of the search.

Stone continued. "Has anyone else, any strangers, come to town the past week and a half? Anyone you don't know who may have abducted the girls?"

Sally answered. "I get people from all over who

come to my store, mainly in the morning and up until about lunchtime. This last week or so has been steady, normal. Maybe ten or fifteen people a day who I don't know, another ten or fifteen regulars."

"What about the churches? How was your service last Sunday? Any new people?"

Pastor Carry spoke up first. "Judge, we're pretty consistent, being that we are the only Black church that I know of south of Miami City proper. Everyone who normally attends, attends. We don't get a lot of new visitors if you understand my meaning. Aren't a lot of Black folk wondering about the Everglades on Sundays looking for salvation." She smiled.

Stone nodded again, then said, "Pastor Rick, what about your service last week?"

"Well, Judge"—Pastor Rick made a big show of thinking about it—"we are consistently growing. I have to think, but it seems last week we maybe had fewer empty pews than the week before. We are starting to draw from Homestead proper..." He trailed off.

"Are there a lot of houses near here, somewhere the girls may have sought shelter?"

Pastor Rick answered. "Not a lot, but not none. Maybe twenty or so within an hour's walk. Twice that within a two-hour walk."

All the other regulars nodded their agreement with his assessment.

Before Stone could speak again, Billy, the older boy, came running back in. "Mister! Mister! It's just like you said. We see vultures! Come look!"

Everyone followed Billy out, even Bahama Bill, coming around the bar, all finished setting up the oil lamps.

As Stone exited, he saw Ron, the younger boy, down at the far end of the walkway. Billy ran past him and stopped by Ron's side, saying something to him excitedly.

Stone approached, scanning the horizon as he did. Then as he got close, way in the distance, he could see the big fat birds circling a spot. It was south, into the Everglades proper.

The sun was setting in the west, the sky starting to turn bloodred. The weather was still cool, suggesting when the sun went down, it would get considerably colder. Florida was no Colorado, but forty degrees in the full wet-humidity was a noticeable temperature drop.

After studying the horizon, once everyone had approached, Stone turned to the group. "Does anyone know if there is anything down there?"

Pastor Rick answered, "No, Judge, it's just all swamp that far south. Going to be extremely hard to get to. I hate to say it, but the night is no time to be wondering about down there."

Laundry sputtered in reply. "Cold will slow the rattlesnakes down. Alligators, too, if they come out of the water. But my girls will be miserable!"

"Better to be miserable, Mayor," Sally Jones said thoughtfully. The others nodded their agreement.

I have to separate out Pastor Rick and not let him go off on his own, Stone thought. *The rest of this crew could end up in trouble out there in the dark. Maybe not the barkeep; he seems a big fellow, but the rest are not trail-ready for sure.*

"Okay, here is what I want to do," Stone said in his old commanding voice, the base in it hanging in the air. "Martha and I will head for the vultures. I have a lot of experience in the wilderness, and Martha grew up in it. Pastor Rick, I want you to stay here with Gary. There is still a chance that the girls will come home. Bill—"

"Bahama Bill," Bahama Bill said.

"Sorry, Bahama Bill, you take Sally and start knocking on doors. Start with the houses closest and work your way out. If the kids got injured or something, it is possible they are being cared for by someone in their home, and they have not been able to leave yet to find their father.

"Sally, if it is okay with you, I would like your boys to stay here. I assume they know Jill, and she knows how to watch them?"

"Yes, that's fine. And yes, I will feel better if they all stay here, so I know they are safe."

Coral was standing next to Ed. "Judge, what do you want Ed and I to do?"

Stone looked from her to Ed. "Ed, if it is okay with you, I would like you and Coral to drive up to Homestead. There is a county sheriff's substation. There should be at least two deputies on duty. Tell him what is going on, and get them to send someone out as soon as they can, no later than tomorrow morning."

Laundry's expression changed. "Well, er, I don't know about Homestead, Ed. Is that the best place to go? I, um, well, I wonder if they could bring a bigger search party?" His emotions were clearly changing a few times; he was worried about his daughters and something else.

Pastor Rick jumped in. "Yes, Homestead. I don't know, Judge. We like to deal with things ourselves out here."

"My girls!" Laundry wheezed. "Yes, please bring help! Homestead is only a few miles away; you can be there in half an hour with your car!"

Pastor Rick made a sour face but did not protest.

I hate the idea of leaving this lot unattended, but Martha and I are the best qualified to look for the two girls in the swamp at night. Once we find them or discover what happened to them, I can deal with this crew here. If this turns out to be the work of IX-Chel, it is going to be the start of some tough times. If not, then we're still dealing with a tragedy.

EVERGLADES

NOVEMBER 22, 1919, 9 P.M.

Stone and Martha continued to walk along the game trails, heading, as best as they could tell, to the general location the vultures had been seen circling. The point of interest was about a mile into the swamp and south, away from the town. They both had changed clothes from their overnight bags, switching from their funeral attire to more practical fittings. Stone had also holstered his Colt Police Positive Special. A long name for a relatively simple thirty-eight caliber revolver.

Bahama Bill, as he insisted on being called, generously provided rooms upstairs in the tavern for Stone and Martha, and for Ed, at no cost.

Martha carried the modified lantern that Bahama Bill had made from the replaced interior tavern lights. It provided enough light to be able to see the ground and a few feet in all directions. She was using the light to examine the dirt paths, tracking what she believed were footprints of a size and weight that could easily be the two Laundry girls.

Stone had decided not to call out for the children—not yet, at least—while letting Martha track. If the trail went dry, maybe. But if they were dealing with nefarious entities, people, or otherwise, he did not want to alert them to their approach. Sound carried much farther at night than their makeshift light.

"Judge," Martha asked after a while.

"Yes, Martha?"

"If we discover that Pastor Rick's church has become a cult of IX-Chel like we talked about, is killing them all really something you would consider?"

Stone looked at her, deciding to tell her the truth about a lot of things he usually kept to himself. If she genuinely represented the possibility of a life partner, she would find out anyway, eventually.

"Done it before, Martha."

"What does that mean? Done it before?" She said the last part imitating his deep bass voice.

"How much of it do you want to know? I don't see the need to drudge all this up now if you are just going back to your camp with your sisters when this is over and if I am going on my way."

She looked him in the eye. "Judge, if we are gearing up for a big honest session here, then there are some things you should know too. I never held much interest in being with anyone. Not just you as a *chikierta,* an outsider, but anyone. Indian men have their own difficulties.

"But there is some connection we share; no way around it. It brings me new feelings. I think I know what they are. I don't know that I like them, and I am trying to decide if I should listen to them."

"I understand, Martha. I think that sums up my current predicament also. My life changed a long time ago, and I let go of the personal side, for good reasons."

"We come from the same place then, it seems. We share a connection that neither of us wants. But Judge, honestly, I don't know if it is a connection in this world or another. I don't know if it is presented to us as a distraction to weaken us or as an opportunity to share and strengthen our resolve.

"I want to show you something. Something I discovered in the sweat lodge that has clouded my judgment, or at least I fear it is clouding my judgment."

Stone wrinkled his brow. "Okay?"

"I have reached over and held your hand a few times, right?"

"Yes."

"Do you know why?"

"Well, no, but I didn't mind it."

"Of course not." She smiled and rolled her eyes. "But it was just a pleasant experience, right?"

"Sure, yes."

"What I discovered is that when we are alone, with no other people around, in the dark, it's different. I tried to help you in the lodge once, alone, when the fire had died down. After that, I always made sure at least one of my sisters was with me."

"I have a vague memory of that, of there being two of you making me drink water."

Martha stopped walking and closed the lantern shade, putting it down. She turned to him, standing a few feet away.

"Everything is normal, correct?"

"Yes."

She took a step closer.

"Still?"

"Yes."

Another step, now very close but not touching. The faintest light started to glow between them. There was not much space, maybe a few inches. The light sparked here and there, shooting back and forth between them, brighter where their bodies were closer.

The light created a feeling of euphoria in both of them, just at the edges, a sense of well-being and optimism.

"Now?" she asked.

"That's amazing." He went to touch her. She recoiled quickly, not allowing the contact, the light immediately fading.

"No, Judge! I know what happens; it's not what you think."

Stone put his hand down, confused. Whatever the reaction between them clouded his thoughts.

"I don't understand. What happens?"

She reached down and opened up the light from the lantern. In the light, both she and Stone were flush.

"What happens is not important until we come to an understanding. So back to my question. If we discover that Pastor Rick's church has become a cult of IX-Chel, is killing them all really something you would consider?"

"Yes, Martha. Like I said, I have done it before. It's part of the deal I made."

"What is this deal? You have mentioned it before. I know some of it, I think. I understand you are now living differently than a normal man.

I know you can see into the spirit world and that they can see you back."

"I'll tell you as best I can," he said. "Some of it, like you said, we live here in reality governed by the spirit world. If you take religion out of it and focus on the foundations, you can start to understand the edges. They are the things that almost all religions share. But I'll give you the truth of it.

"There are four realms. The lowest is our world here. This is also the most real sphere and the only one where the physical has more sway than the spiritual. But we're also the most important. Everything starts here, and what goes on in the physical world greatly influences what goes on in the spiritual realms. This is why it seems like we are in a constant state of manipulation and consequence.

"Because we are.

"This is where spirits are made and formed. This world is a big machine, a giant circular wheel, a factory for spirits. Souls come and go. Time is the power that turns the wheel. The wheel produces souls for the other realms."

He looked at her; they had stopped walking. "Do you understand?" he asked.

"Yes."

"Do you believe?"

"Yes. The number four is sacred in native beliefs. It makes sense there are four realms," Martha said while nodding her head.

"So then the question is what happens to our souls when they leave the physical realm? I can explain how we are bound here later if you wish, but it's not a key to understanding the deal I made."

"That's fine."

"When we die, our spirits transition to one of the three other realms, based upon both what we believe and what we did with our time here in the physical world. So just to be clear, you and I have discussed different religions. None of them are correct, and none of them are wrong. They each just provide a way for our human brains to conceptualize and deal with these concepts that would otherwise be too big for our understanding.

"The other realms are, using Christian concepts, Heaven, Purgatory, and Hell. Using common language, they are the desired place (Heaven), the undesired place (Hell), and the safe place (Purgatory).

"A Christian won't like Purgatory called the safe place. They like the idea of punishment and reward. Correct me, but natives are the opposite; you don't believe there is a punishment involved in death," Stone said as he looked at Martha already knowing the answer.

"That's right."

"But you also don't have vital concepts of three realms in Indian religions. You believe in the physical, and then pretty much the universe, or the sky, as you said once. That's purgatory.

"But it is, of course, a lot more complicated in all that; I am just trying to frame some of this. Each religion has some elements correct and some elements wrong.

"In its simplest form, death is a filter. It is applied by the shadows of the other side, the shadows of the different realms. They are another complicated topic we can discuss later. The shadows have their own hierarchy and concepts.

"What they try and do is match the soul as it transitions from the physical world and to direct it to the realm that it is best suited for. Christianity isn't entirely wrong in its outcomes. Generally speaking, bad people go to the undesirable place, and good people go to the desirable place. Purgatory is for people who are about equal parts good and bad. Which are most people."

The trail they were on came to a fork. Martha studied the ground. "One child went this way, and one child went that way," she said, indicating the two possible directions.

"Let's follow the younger one."

Martha studied some more, then indicated the

left trail.

Stone continued. "So there is a lot more to it, but let me explain the deal. What is interesting is that everyone who is able to go to the desirable place is offered this same deal. Billions of souls in the history of the universe have been offered the deal. I'm the only one who ever said yes to it."

There was a rustling to the side. Stone stopped talking; both he and Martha listened. Martha quickly shut the sides of the light; they stood in the dark, cold night.

The rustling came again, along with guttural growling.

"It's an alligator, a big one. That's a mating call," Martha said, backing away from the direction of the sound.

Stone acted on instinct, drawing his revolver and firing several rounds into the brush in the direction of the noise. There was the wet sound of an impact followed by the noise of a large animal moving away.

As the gunshot report faded, a call came in on the wind.

"Hello?"

Stone reloaded his handgun and holstered it.

The voice came again. "Hello? Who is there?" It sounded like a little girl, mostly. There was a hollowness to the call that rang through.

"Judge, look!" Martha called out, pointing to a faint white light about a hundred feet down the trail.

A little girl was giving off the light, a beacon in the darkness. She looked to be about twelve, so this would be Lara. It was clear she was a spirit; her features were just the slightest malformed. She was wearing a bonnet, and frilly dress, like a little girl would wear to church on Sunday.

Stone saw the spirit but did not move to it. "Martha, please stand behind me. I am sure this is the spirit we believe it is. However, children's spirits are rare; they have little need to be earthbound."

She stepped behind him. "I don't understand; we just worked with Eric's spirit."

"He was eighteen. That's an adult."

The little girl spirit saw them and began moving toward them. It was a combination of walking and just moving.

"Are you the judge? I am supposed to find the judge."

"What is your name, little one?" Stone said once the spirit was close.

"Lara Laundry. My name rhymes."

"Why didn't you go to the light?"

The spirit stopped, and its features changed.

The dress turned red with blood in places.

"There was no light, Judge."

"How did you die?"

"Judge, I can see things. Things I don't understand. I see you, and I see both darkness and light. There is a brighter light behind you, a woman. An Indian. But her light doesn't lead anywhere."

Stone stiffened. The presence of Martha was confusing this spirit also, just like Eric's spirit had been confused.

"How did you die?" he asked again. Spirits were tricky; they weren't all good. Even a child's spirit could redirect you, could distract you from doing the right thing or seeing all the choices.

The girl's dress turned even bloodier; it looked like fresh wounds were opening up.

"I got eaten, I guess. It hurts, Judge. It keeps happening. It's happening again. I thought you were supposed to help! That's what they said."

Martha made an empathetic sound and started to move from behind Stone. He reached his arm out to keep her behind him.

"Wait," he said low so only Martha could hear.

The little girl started to cry, then scream in fear, then scream in pain, then wail in agony. It went on for some time, the dress flowing red, bite marks appearing on her neck and face. After a few moments, something happened to her legs; they came apart just under the knees, separated. The little spirit fell, giving off now an ungodly uproar of pain and suffering that filled the night air.

Martha yelled, upset, "We have to do something!" She grew angry at Stone's inaction.

"Wait," he said again, still with his arm out to prevent Martha from advancing on the spirit.

The night went dark, and the noise from the spirit gurgled out. They stood in complete silence and darkness.

"Stop blocking me!" Martha yelled, now fully angry at Stone.

"Wait," he said again. "This is an echo of what happened. It will repeat forever unless we figure out what Lara needs to find rest. You can't interfere; if you interfere, she may become confused, and we could lose her."

"I thought the whole point of your deal, whatever it is, is to interfere!"

"The point is to help." He allowed his own anger and frustration to come out, the low echo in his voice conveying power and experience. It was enough to shake Martha out of her rage and remind her that she witnessed events that Stone knew a great deal about.

After another good while, a small light formed

over the spot where Lara's spirit had fallen.

It took several minutes, the light eventually brightening until it revealed that Lara was standing there, just as before, her bonnet and dress looking fresh.

"Judge," Lara said, "do you know where my father is? I miss him."

"I do, little one. But I need to know more. You said you were eaten. I need to know why. Was it an alligator out here in the swamp?"

Lara shook her head. "No, it was a monster, like a dog with big horns. There was a lady there too. She drew a circle around me; it kept the light away. I screamed and screamed in the night, but no one ever came to help."

Stone turned to Martha. "You mentioned that other symbol to me, the sign of an arc in the dirt with two lines through it. Could that be used in this way?"

"Yes," she said, calm again, understanding a bit more about how the spirit world worked. It was deeper and more complicated than she realized, even though she had dabbled at its edges as a medicine woman for most of her life.

Stone turned back to Lara. "Child, I can help you. We need to remove that symbol near your body where you passed."

The little spirit started to bleed red from under

her dress again. "Follow me, Judge. I'll take you to my body. I hope you have a strong tummy," the spirit said as it started to whimper from the pain again.

**

Ed drove with Coral in his Model 31. She was sitting all the way over near him, leaning into him, even though there was plenty of room on the front seat bench.

"Ed, this is the most fantastic car!" she squealed as they drove away, grabbing his arm in excitement.

"All I did was buy it; it's just a machine." Ed did not get satisfaction out of trying to impress someone with acquisitions. What was the point? He didn't build the car.

"Why did you switch from your old one?" Coral asked being very curious since the car was so impressive.

"I wanted something that had a sturdier frame and roof. Something that was safer." All the truth, just lacking the context.

"Well, I think it is lovely. What a luxury! Do you know this is only the third time I have ever even been in a car?"

Ed turned to look at her then got his eyes back firmly on the road. "What were the other two times?" His practical brain focused on the details, not the corollary the statement was probably meant to elicit.

"Ha! Oh Ed, you never fail to surprise me. I do have something I found out, though, that I need to tell you." She was already leaning in close; she put her hand on Ed's knee when she spoke.

Ed looked down at the hand. It made him uncomfortable. "Could you move over on the bench? I appreciate the closeness, but I need to focus on driving. It is very dark out, and these roads are not very good."

Coral made her pouting face, pushing her bottom lip out. Ed had become familiar with the gesture; it was losing its impact on him. But she scooted over, not losing her enthusiasm.

"So Ed, I found out something about Mayor Laundry. It is hard to talk bad about him since his two little girls are missing, but I'm worried he doesn't have your best interest at heart!"

That's an odd statement, two little girls. Betty is fifteen, and Coral is twenty. Not peers, but not terribly far apart in age.

To Coral, he said, "What do you mean?" He tried not to show that he suspected anything, but of course, he knew that the whole setup was a grift.

"I heard him talking to Pastor Rick. It took me a few minutes to understand what they were discussing, but he told the Pastor that he didn't really run the ads for the land in the paper like he said he would. He said it didn't matter, and he didn't want to alert anyone.

"At first, I thought he was trying to help you. To help you buy the land without any competition, to keep the price of the land low. But then Pastor Rick said that he had found a printer who could make a fake deed!

"Did you hear me, Ed? A fake deed! What does that mean?"

Should I act surprised?

She is lying, Ed!

Oh no. No, no, no, no. Voice, go away. I thought you were gone with your other believers!

Ed started to sweat even though the night was cool.

"Ed, are you okay? I didn't mean to shock you!" Coral was looking at him, concerned.

She is lying, Ed! How could she know that? She is in on the trick! She doesn't love you like I do!

Now you love me again, Voice?

Use my name, Ed. It sounds so lovely when you say it.

No! You are the voice, that's it. And you are bad! Look what you did to that boy; you are lucky I didn't see him like you wanted.

Ed, if you could have seen the glorious work, you

would believe in me forever.

"Ed, answer me! Stop the car; something is wrong. The look on your face is scaring me!"

Who is talking? Is Coral upset?

"Coral, calm down. I'm used to being by myself. I usually think a lot when I drive."

Ed slowed the car down but didn't stop.

What did she tell me?

Oh silly, am I the only one listening? She told you that the fat mayor is trying to scam you!

Why are you talking so nice to me again?

Oh, Ed. I can't fool you, can I. No one can fool you! I thought I had found a new flock, but their belief is weak. It is going to unravel. It hasn't yet, but I know the signs. You are the only one that truly believes in me. I was wrong to think otherwise. I love you so much! These others try harder than you, and they do awful things if I tell them to! They are so corruptible. That's not satisfying, not like having you around. I can't corrupt you; you are pure!

"Ed, I am serious. Stop the car and talk to me!" Coral was starting to cry.

Ed stopped the car and looked at her.

"I heard you; I'm trying to process what you said. The mayor and the pastor are in cahoots to try and defraud me."

I would never try and trick you, Ed!

Shut up, you! You are a liar; you have tried to trick me many times.

Oh, Ed. You misunderstand; I would never try! I apologize; I have deceived you on occasion before, yes. But I didn't try. I simply did it!

"Ed," Coral said, "you know I would never try and trick you like they did, right? You know I didn't know anything about it!" Coral started sobbing very loudly, almost too loudly. The emotion seemed exaggerated.

The voice started laughing. Ed was accosted with sensory overload. Coral weeping loudly, the voice laughing maniacally, both ringing in his head.

Shut up, you!

"Coral, stop crying!" Ed demanded to no avail.

The voice continued to laugh; Coral continued to cry.

Shut up! Shut up!

"Shut up! Shut up!" he screamed both in his head and out loud.

Coral recoiled in horror as Ed screamed at her, her sobs becoming more pronounced, maybe more real.

"What's wrong with you! How can you talk to me that way?"

Yes Ed, what's wrong with you? How can you talk to

me that way!

More laughing and more crying.

Ed came unglued. He couldn't get away from the noise, he couldn't think, he couldn't make it stop. The voice was so loud and relentless, and Coral was screaming at him something about taking her back home.

Then from nowhere, the sound of scraping on the outside of the car brought immediate silence. It was a terrifying sound, slow and methodical. Somehow the sound of bone on metal sounded longing, like it wanted something, and was full of anticipation.

Coral's screams and tears shifted from anger to fear. Her eyes wide.

"Ed! Oh my god, oh my god. I can see it. It's a monster!" Now she was frantic and flailing about in the seat, pushing herself away from the window and all the way into his lap.

Ed gathered himself at the last minute, slipped the car into gear, and smashed the accelerator all the way to the floor.

***

The little spirit of Lara led Stone and Martha through the Everglades. The temperature had dropped to the low forties; it was legitimately cold. Dampness hung in the night air, and there was enough of a breeze to make everything feel unpleasant.

The girl's body had been tied down, similar to Eric Adams's body. However, it looked like the stakes had been moved a couple times. The tiny form had clearly been on the ground for a while, possibly over a week. Its legs were broken below the knee, indicating horrible suffering, but it was the state of the rest of it that told the true horror.

Had the remains been fresh, it might have been more than Stone or Martha could stand, looking at it. The week of decay helped to dehumanize it some. Still, the tiny, skinny body of the little girl brought feelings of rage at its mistreatment. It was hard to tell what happened; vultures had been working on it for several days now.

The eyes were gone, picked out, along with most of the face. Some of the original fatal bite marks could still be seen. They were not as specific as Eric's, although eventually, it looked like the same areas had been targeted.

"Why did they break your legs?" Martha asked the spirit, sounding motherly and caring.

Without hesitation, the spirit replied, "I kept running away. The monster that was trying to hold me didn't have steady hands. It took them a while, but I managed to escape a couple of times. I didn't get all that far, and after the second time, the bigger one, the really mean one, she smashed a rock on me until my legs broke. It hurt a great deal."

"I'm sorry this happened to you," Martha said in response.

Stone was looking around. Eventually, he found something that looked like the symbol Martha had drawn for him earlier at the car.

"Martha, over here. It is just as you thought." He pointed to the symbol on the ground. After she looked at it, he started to wipe it away with his foot.

"No, Judge. Wait." She put a hand on his shoulder to emphasize the point.

He paused, watching her.

She started to walk the area, studying the ground, using the oil lamp as best she could to see. "Help me look around; we need to make sure there are no other symbols first. Then we can undo these and bless the child."

They looked for a few minutes. Lara stood right next to her mangled and battered body, a soft white light surrounding her. She did not have the spells where the wounds reappeared during this time.

"Okay, it's just the one," Martha said eventually. "It feels to me like this is the first time they tried the ritual. The body is too mangled. The whole site is very unsophisticated. I expected other wards, some protection for them from the spirit world."

Stone stood back and looked at everything. "Laundry is running a scam on Ed. We think the pastor is transitioning his church into a cult. They seem to be working together, but I don't get the feeling that Laundry knows about the cult, do you?"

Martha stood up and walked over so she could have the same perspective Stone did on the scene. "No parent would do this to their child. And no parent could spend a second in the same room as someone who did."

"The question becomes, does Pastor Rick know this was done? Does he understand the forces he has aligned himself with?"

She turned to look him in the eyes. "Does it matter? He made this possible." She composed herself. "Judge, I was wrong about you."

He made a face of surprise. "Really? How so?"

"I doubted your actions. I told myself I could not be with a person willing to kill people to stop a spirit. I was convinced that you were wrong, that you were too brutal a man for me. I thought my morals were superior to yours."

He looked back to the mutilated scene and the mangled body of the little girl, gesturing with his head. "But now?"

"Now I have different feelings. I would want to kill anyone responsible for this, but I do not believe

I have the fortitude to do it. Killing is hard. But you do. I know it; I have seen it in your eyes and watched it in your actions. When I look at you now, I see strength and resolve, a willingness to do the hard work."

Stone nodded. He was sad that she now saw him this way but knew it was the truth of things. After a time of standing there, she reached over and took his hand. He welcomed it, and they stood together for a while.

Finally, Martha released his hand. "I can purify the scene, undo the marker, and we can get Lara here on to her rewards."

The wind picked up.

"You do that; I'll figure out how to dig a grave." He looked away, then a thought struck him. "Martha, you know what they say?"

"What's that, Judge?" She started her preparations.

"Everyone wants to get into heaven, but there are a whole lot fewer who are willing to do the work."

PALM STREET TAVERN

NOVEMBER 23, 1919, JUST AFTER MIDNIGHT

As the dim lights of Florida City came into view, Coral had calmed down. The voice had stopped its yammering.

Ed's subconscious was screaming something at him, something obvious. He knew it was there but feared allowing the thought to form into words in his consciousness for concern of the voice hearing it. He had worked most of the drive back to keep the idea out of his head. Finally, somehow, it came into clarity without having to be transposed by his internal dialog.

He slowed the car.

"Coral?"

"Yes, Ed? I'm sorry I freaked out; that was terrifying. What was that thing back there?"

"Do you think we should turn around and try and get to the county sheriff's office like we are supposed to?"

Something flashed across her face, very different from the typical jovial and warm looks she often gave him. "I thought we agreed to go back home?"

"Sure, yes. And, yes, that was very scary with the owl monster right outside the car. But don't we owe it to Mayor Laundry? To his kids? To try and get help?"

He stopped the car. The lights and buildings of Florida City were clearly visible but still in the distance, maybe a half-mile away.

Coral was frantically thinking. "Yes, I want to help him. But that thing out there! How is us getting killed by it going to help anyone?" She was becoming overly frantic.

Ed pressed the accelerator and turned the car back in the direction of the sheriff.

He fed his own thoughts to try something, a lie.

Gee, I sure hope she understands how important this is!

Nothing. As the car completed its turn, he accelerated.

"Ed, seriously, take me home first. I don't want to go anymore. I'm too scared!" Coral said as she started to panic.

Again. *Gee, I sure hope she understands how important this is!*

She will never understand that, Ed!

What should I do with her, Voice? Should we sacrifice her?

"Ed!" She grabbed his shoulder and shook him. "Take me home!"

Voice, let's do it! Let's cut her into pieces!

Edward. Yes, of course, that's the plan. But I need to prepare a place first. Then we can do it.

So, not now, but later? Promise?

Yes! The place we can prepare is back in town. Let's go there now!

Coral continued to yell in the car, and the voice got louder in his head.

Ed nodded to himself, slowed the car, and turned it back around. It was just as he suspected.

Coral's mood changed, again; she slid over in the seat and kissed his cheek. "Oh, thank you, Ed! I knew you were one of the good guys!"

The voice stopped its yammering, again, and was gone, again.

Coral allowed her hand to rest on Ed's knee, then moved it a little closer up his leg. "Ed, you deserve a reward!"

Ed turned to look at her. In the dark car, she

looked very young. He had forgotten just how long ago he had been twenty years old. Her advances and interest in him did not make any sense until now. He felt it all along but had not allowed himself to face the fact.

"Let's get back to the tavern. You can stay in my room tonight if you want to," he said, still playing his game. Ed knew he had to start taking charge. He knew the town was playing him for a fool, maybe a rich fool at that. They were running a con, a long con. Ed was no novice; he needed to start turning the tables.

Coral, it seemed, had the role of either the roper or the shill. The roper's job was to get close to the mark and bring him in, the shill to seem disconnected from the grift but provide encouragement and legitimacy. No, the shill was that old lady secretary. Coral had transitioned from the roper to the face; her job was now to keep Ed interested. What better way to keep a small, old, lonely, outsider immigrant interested than a young woman and the promise of a family, acceptance, and good life?

Ed allowed his brain to process the information; now that the mental barrier had been broken, it flooded through. He didn't allow an internal dialog, the voice would hear that, but he could think it through nonetheless. He decided the actual grift was being run by Mayor Laundry and Pastor Rick, even though the pastor may have been brought in after the fact as the voice began to interfere.

Or maybe Bahama Bill. He was a big scary man who stayed in the shadows, on the edges. He had killed a lot of people when he was a Rough Rider. He controlled Coral. Oh no, Ed realized. He controlled Coral!

Coral was beaming with what looked like pride. "Ed, I will! Oh, terrific. We are going to have so much fun tonight!"

If she was the face, her job for the past couple of months had been to get Ed to commit to a relationship with her so she could have better control of him. She must have been getting pressure from Bahama Bill since Ed had been deflecting her advances as quickly as they came at him. He surmised her weird turn of emotions and current excitement that was coming from her, finally fulfilling her end of the grift.

"Yes," Ed said. "Tonight is going to be a barrel of monkeys for sure."

***

Stone and Martha walked back, the task completed; Lara had ascended and was at peace.

"Judge, I would like to understand the rest of your deal. We kind of got interrupted there."

They held hands with the gas lantern open and turned up as high as it could go. Stone was covered in mud and dirt. He dug Lara's grave using only his hands and tools he could make from rocks and whatever else he could find nearby. It was difficult to work, but he was built for it, and the ground was mostly sand.

Martha continued her question. "You said that every soul in Heaven is offered a choice when they arrive, but that none take it. None except for you. What is the choice? Why did you accept it?"

Stone paused. Martha stopped a few feet farther up the path. It took so much energy to try and go through this. He had explained it to Jack Abbott after Jack died and came back. Jack was a spirit at the time with a much better perspective, and it *still* took a lot of energy to get him to fully understand.

"Okay, Martha. I will try and tell you. I am not going to try and explain it to you. It would take too long. You can work through it with me later; there is a lifetime of conversation here, more. But, I agree it is fair that you know, so you have some idea what you are getting into.

"So, like I said, I'll tell you. You probably will want to challenge the ideas; they seem simple to us here in the physical world."

Her interest was piqued. "Okay, I will just listen as best I can."

"You can ask questions. I'm just saying that we are not going to have the time to really get into a lot of it."

"Sure."

"Okay. I'll use the Christian terms just to keep it simple, but just the terms. We can discuss both Christian and native beliefs. Others too, if they come into play. I'll also tell you that there are some things I don't know. I don't know a lot of the whys. Why things work the way they do, why the other realms need souls, why everything is tied in through the physical world. I simply don't know. I can tell you what I suspect if you want."

"Yes, of course, please," Martha said as curiosity turned to intrigue.

"I suspect we are all part of a system that was put in place a long time ago. I mean a really long time ago, like before the sky even existed, to use the Indian perspective. It is clear to me that whatever this system of four realms is, and the way things flow between them, that this is part of some other arrangement. But we'll never understand the whole thing; even just trying to understand the pieces we can interact with, the elements that affect us, is challenging.

"So, I suspect that no one knows why any of this works the way it does. There is no intelligence left in existence that was part of the creation. Not our design, not the 'And God said let there be light!' creation, but the making of the structure itself, the whole structure. What we call gods are just beings from the other realms. They have more power and influence here—wait, that's wrong. They have more power here, but the influence can be balanced.

"But they don't know the whys any more than we do.

"I also know there is some type of competition for souls. Souls are a resource that each realm covets. The only way to influence which domain a soul goes to is by manipulating what we do as people and exploiting what we believe as individuals. What we believe comes from our experiences here in the physical world.

"There seems to be some controls built-in, some semblance of how much influence is allowed from the outer realms to the physical one, and how much direct manipulation is possible. The system, though, is mostly self-regulating. And, there are no ways for the shadows to arbitrate disputes between themselves. Well, there are ways, but I mean there is no arbitrator to go to. The shadows basically devolve into fighting when there is a dispute."

"I don't understand what you mean by dispute?" Martha said furrowing her brow in trying to understand.

"Sure. The problem with all of this is that everything is pretty subjective, right? Good souls go to Heaven, bad souls go to Hell, most souls go to Purgatory. But what is good and bad?"

He paused, having been through this explanation a few times and knowing that this was one of the more challenging conceptual steps for a person to take. It helped if they took the journey step-by-step.

Martha realized he meant the question to be answered. "We Indians know this answer, Judge. It's maybe where we are closer to the truth. A person is good when they behave and are careful about how they use their own power. We would say that brings balance. When they do not behave or if they use their power recklessly, they are out of balance."

Stone smiled. "That's right, I had forgotten. It is not considered a struggle between good and evil in native customs; it is about the balance itself. About being in balance or out of balance."

"Yes."

"But there is still a lot to unpack there. Who decides what balance is? Who decides what it means to behave?"

"Indians know this already, Judge. The teachings come from our ancestors. They are traditions."

Stone's smile faded. "Martha, you are smart, and I respect you and your ancestors. But I am about to change some of your perspectives if we continue. Are you sure you want to? You won't be able to see things the same after. I mean your people, your customs."

Martha made a face like this was not possible. "I doubt that, Judge. But, I am curious why you think it to be true, so yes, please, let's continue."

They had resumed slowly walking back to town and were close enough now to see the low lights. Martha stopped; if they got any closer, their voices would start to carry. There was a large rock near the trail they were on; Stone waked over and sat on it, tired from the work of digging the grave without any real tools. Martha sat down on the rock next to him, leaning against his side. She dimmed the lantern but did not dampen it. They were awash in the low yellow glow of the oily light.

When everything was settled, Stone continued. "There is a hierarchy to the different realms. Again, I don't know why or how, just that it is so. Heaven has dominion over Hell. Hell has dominion over Purgatory.

"As you reminded me, natives don't see the afterlife as a reward or punishment. You see it as returning to the sky, what I would call the universe. I said that this was a view of Purgatory. You didn't react then, but I want to use this to explain how things are. You say knowing balance and imbalance come from your ancestors. But where did they learn it?"

She considered the question, a few thoughts working their way into her thinking. She started to realize where Stone was going.

"Oh," she said.

Stone put his hand on her shoulder. He wanted to embrace her more but knew that this was not the time. He knew that she was about to be confronted with a truth she had not expected. He remained quiet, letting her work through it, opening the door for her to say it back to him as she processed the information.

"We have been designed to populate Purgatory. They tricked us!"

He continued to wait.

Martha went on. "If what you say is true—"

"It is true," he interrupted. This was often the first step, denial, and then challenge. "I told you that you would want to contest the truth of it." He allowed some edge in his voice, he spoke with authority, and his knowledge was accurate. He could see she was working very hard not to simply dismiss the information; instead trying to see where it went.

"But why?"

"I told you I don't know the why of it."

"Why would a whole people be denied Heaven?"

"You're not denied it; that's not how it works. But, just a few moments ago, you proudly announced that natives didn't even believe in

Heaven!" He knew this was dangerous ground.

"I want to be angry, but I don't know why." She looked over to him, searching his eyes for something. For some answer or context that wasn't there. "You are telling me that things work exactly as I thought. Exactly as I was brought up. You're confirming it with firsthand knowledge, something that is impossible. Yet, somehow, I feel like I have been betrayed! Not by you, but by...I don't even know what.

"I could right now take this information back to an elder, and they would be happy with it. If they accepted it as truth, they could rest easy knowing they are correct in their beliefs in spirits, and in the sky, and in what our ancestors have taught them. That they are doing exactly the right things to get the outcome they want!"

Stone stayed silent, as did Martha for a few moments. Then Stone continued.

"I didn't tell you that to challenge your beliefs, mind you. I'm just trying to get to the deal I made."

She nodded understanding.

"So," he resumed, "what is interesting about Christianity is that they pursue Heaven, but because of that pursuit, many more of them go to Hell. Natives work for balance, and in so doing, by and large, receive the outcome they want. Christians work for Heaven and, by and large, don't make it.

"But Martha, I want to be clear. Many natives go to Heaven, far more than you may realize. By striving for balance, they end up leading a better life than someone tempted by the possibility of a reward for their actions and beliefs. People are a funny lot, and they act and consider some unhelpful things sometimes."

"So Judge"—Martha wanted to get to the heart of it—"I think I understand most of that. You were right; there is a lot I want to discuss with you. I have a thousand questions. But given all this, what is the deal you made?"

Stone looked her in the eye. "I gave up my place in Heaven to be able to work here on Earth to try and keep good people out of Hell."

Martha stared back at him for a good while, trying to process the information. She wanted to avoid the obvious question, but it was the only thought she had.

"Why?" she asked.

"I don't have time to explain it now, but I promise I will as we continue our journey together. It is a simple answer, but also a complicated one."

"I can imagine." Martha said, eye wide and moving from side to side.

"However, I still need to explain what it means."

"Right, because you came back."

"Yes." Stone thought inwardly for a second,

reflecting on something. "I came back; I am not the same as before."

"So what exactly do you do? You started out by saying that there is no mediator, no arbitrator in the spirit world, yet there seem to be rules and controls. Is that why you call yourself Judge? Are you an arbitrator?"

"I call myself Judge because I was one for a very long time. It became who I am, how I think, even though I was betrayed by those that sought my guidance. But that is another story. The simple answer is that no, I am not a judge for the spirit world. I actually hold no sway in the other realms whatsoever.

"I have an opportunity here, on Earth, to do something that I find much more important than judging spirits. I have the chance to help them."

"How can you help spirits?" Martha asked even though she had seen him operate with Lara and Eric.

"This part is also complicated, so I will just hit the edges of it. Remember I said that spirits go where they fit best? That good people go to the good place, bad people to the bad place. Those who were both good and bad, which is most of us, they go to Purgatory.

"Well, when a person dies, how they are perceived on the other side has a lot to do with how they perceive themselves. It might not sound fair, but it is how it works. I don't know the 'whys,' as I mentioned. If a spirit feels good about what it did in life, that counts on the scale.

"Now, I already know your first question. Go ahead." He could see she wanted to ask something. It was always the same question, and he always gave the same answer.

"So if I do bad things, don't behave, lead a very unbalanced life, maybe even kill people for no reason. But if I feel good about it, if I believe I was justified in my actions, I'll go to Heaven even though I acted badly?"

Stone nodded in the affirmative; this was always what got asked. Every time by everyone. "That's a part of it, yes. It's not like you say, exactly, but yes, your self-image is a significant factor in how the other side sees your soul. But it's not simple like your question. First, you have to really believe that you are acting right. You can't just think it, or want to believe it, or work every day to convince yourself.

"It has to be part of your true motivation. The actual driver for your actions. You have to have decided to do whatever you did in life out of a desire to do good."

"Why?"

"I told you, I don't know."

"Judge, that seems terribly unfair!"

Stone laughed a real laugh. He was not expecting to, but the statement truly caught him off-guard.

When he stopped after just a moment, he said, "I know, Martha. I know. It has kept me up at night at times too. But what I learned is that fairness has nothing to do with any of this. Plus, after you really think about it, you will see, I suspect, because I eventually understood. I think it turns out that this is actually a much more fair system of measure than some other way."

"I can't see that from here, that's for sure!" She was animated.

Stone went back into his methodical approach. "But think about it. If you live your whole life trying to do the right thing. How can that detract from your eternal salvation? Why would the judgments of others affect *your* spirit in an afterlife?"

"Because right is right and wrong is wrong! Good is good, Judge. The concepts are universal!" Martha said, slightly exasperated and frustrated at the same time.

"Are they, Martha? Are you sure about that?"

"Yes. Absolutely sure. You can't convince me otherwise."

Stone shook his head; he hated to have to go through all this. Partially because of the effort it took for him not to get angry, partly because it was always difficult to watch a person he liked lose a little bit of faith when confronted with a few simple truths.

"Okay, Martha. Let me give you an example. I'll keep it theoretical, but we can use real examples too, later, if you want."

"That's fine."

"So let's say one person hunts down someone and shoots them in the back at night without warning. Is that a good thing or a bad thing? How should that be judged in the spirit world?"

Martha made a face; her eye twitched a little as she thought. "I want to say that being a back shooter is wrong, but since I know you a little, I know there might be more to it."

"More to it?"

"Yes. I guess I would need to know why they shot them in the back."

"What for? You just said that right is right and wrong is wrong. That the concept of good is universal. Isn't getting shot in the back a pretty specific thing?"

She shook her head. "Okay, I'll play along. Shooting someone in the back is wrong unless they were justified somehow."

"What!?!" Stone pretended with mock outrage. "So what a person does isn't always just good or bad? You just two minutes ago told me the opposite. And you proclaimed I couldn't convince you otherwise!"

Martha smirked, understanding the trap. "Are you going to be a jerk about this all the way through?" It was stated playful enough.

"Ain't no other way." Stone said with a smile on his face.

She was more curious than mad. "Okay, so give me the context."

"I'm making the story up. The context could be anything. But you see the point. How could the evaluation of good or bad, justice or injustice, right or wrong, be made without knowing more about the event? Think about it. If you were really trying to figure this out, what would you do next?"

"You mean if I were a spirit judge?"

"There are not any spirit judges," Stone said quickly.

"I remember. So if I was trying to figure this out, I would want to know what led up to the shooting."

"How would you do that?"

"I guess I would have to ask the person that did the shooting and the person who got shot." She winced, seeing the contradiction, knowing where this probably went.

"Huh." Stone pretended to be stumped. "That would mean we needed to know what they thought they were doing, what each person believed about their actions? That sounds like crazy talk!"

"Ok, smartypants, I see it. And I know that we could change the story to support all kinds of conclusions. Can I take it the whole thing is like this?"

"Yep." He stood up.

"So it's just what you said. It's simple and complicated, and as you understand, the way you see things changes. Ideas and principles you may have lived your life by come into better view. And, even if what you believe still holds, your perspective on its significance could change," she said.

"Yep."

"I don't like it. I understand more, but I feel less confident now." Martha said as she looked at the ground.

He offered her his hand to help her stand up from the rock. "So to finish, if a spirit is sent to me, and I don't mean these kids we have been helping, that's easy. But if a soul is sent to me for help, I have to understand them well enough to help them see themselves in a more positive light.

"If they are sent to me, it is because they are

right on the edge of Hell and Purgatory. If they can understand themselves and gain perspective, often, not always, but often, they are saved from spending an eternity in Hell."

A thought occurred to Martha. "What about Jack Abbott?"

Stone got an irritated look. "I knew Jack most of his life. If anyone deserves real justice in the afterlife, it's Jack. He was good in every meaning of the term. I am not going to help him transition to Purgatory. Before this is all over, I am going to find a way to let him ascend to Heaven."

***

Ed and Coral ran into the tavern.

Pastor Rick and Mayor Laundry were sitting down inside. They stopped what looked like a heated conversation when they saw Ed and Coral enter.

"Is Bahama Bill here?" Coral asked, sounding excited.

"What? No, he and Sally are still out, going house to house," Pastor Rick said. Both he and Laundry had an odd pale look to them. Laundry looked pasty and upset. If possible, he looked more upset than he should have.

Wait, I thought the baker lady, Sally, her kids stayed here? Ed realized after a moment.

"Where are Billy and Ron? Where is the young

woman Jill?" Ed asked.

Laundry made a whimpering noise and looked at his hands, tears streaming.

Pastor Rick responded immediately with a lot of passion. "What! I don't know! We don't know, I mean. How would we know? They left."

"Weren't you two supposed to watch them?" Ed said, shocked. He looked at Coral for reassurance but got a look of confusion back instead. He couldn't read what it meant.

"No!" Pastor Rick yelled. "It's not our fault. What were we supposed to do?"

Coral started to get nervous. "Where is Bahama Bill? I need to talk to him."

This is bad news!

Ed realized the situation was unstable and much worse than he thought.

Pastor Rick gave the kids up! I bet Laundry agreed to it for his kids too. What the hell is wrong with these people? Coral obsessing over Bahama Bill. I was right about the grift; this proves it. I wonder what else there is that I don't know?

His instincts were to run away. It wasn't that he was a coward. Well, he was, but that didn't mean the instinct was wrong. As a small man, flight was a practical option in many situations. He didn't really stand a chance of punching his way out of a jam.

He fought his instinct. "When did it take Billy and Ron?"

Laundry broke down, weeping. "She said I could have Betty back in exchange for the two boys!"

The statement hung in the air. It sounded twisted and sick. Even Laundry reacted when he heard how it sounded out loud.

"We couldn't have done anything anyway!" Pastor Rick screamed. "It wasn't like we had a choice in all this."

Ed snapped, his own fear turning to anger. "Of course you had a choice! You could have tried! Tried anything!"

Pastor Rick shouted back, "It was a monster, Ed! We couldn't have stopped it. It wouldn't have mattered at all!"

"You could have tried, sir!" Ed exclaimed, his pent-up rage and frustration boiling to the surface all at once. "When were they taken?"

Another thought occurred to Ed, everything now flooding in. He turned to Coral. "Where is your room? Back here behind the bar?"

"What?" She was shaking. "Yes. No. Wait, don't go in there!"

Ed stormed over around the bar and pushed open the door to the area that Bahama Bill and Coral shared. He had always assumed it led to a small apartment but never had the chance to look.

As the door opened, it was what he had realized, not what he had hoped. It was just a single room, and there was only one bed.

Coral stood frozen on the other side of the bar. "Ed, it's not what you think!"

"And what do I think, Coral? Do I think that Bahama Bill didn't adopt you? You're not his daughter; you are his wife! What sick twisted game are you all playing?"

Ed! You are so bright. I was going to tell you when I got a chance! She is bad news.

I'll get to you, Voice. Your reckoning is coming, too. Do not hurt those children; I am warning you!

"It's not like that!" Coral yelled. Even Pastor Rick and Mayor Laundry seemed shocked at Ed's revelation about Bahama Bill and Coral.

Pastor Rick looked at Coral hard. "It's not like what, Coral?" A look of confusion and revulsion formed on his face.

Coral became indignant. "Don't judge me, you hack. I am going to go get Bahama Bill; he will put you in your holier-than-thou place!"

She turned and ran out before Ed could get back around the bar to confront her. He called after her. "Coral, wait! It's not safe out there!"

What a mess, Ed! You know I am going to have to devour her soul, right?

Ed was very perplexed. "Pastor," he said, forcing himself to be brave and to not just go get in his car and drive away.

Pastor Rick had been staring at the tavern door Coral exited as though it had some answer.

"Yes, Ed?"

I don't know what to ask him. I am tired of all the mystery and conspiracy. I'll just ask him straight away.

"Pastor, have you turned away from God and are now worshiping a giant white owl?"

That sounded really stupid, Ed.

Aw nuts, is that my voice or the other one?

Either way, it does sound odd out loud.

But Pastor Rick didn't act like it was an odd question. Just the opposite. His eyes got big, and he started to stutter, for all indications caught off guard that Ed knew the truth.

Then Ed saw the look in Pastor Rick's eyes. Cold terror shot down his spine. Pastor Rick had a voice in his head; he was having an internal dialog with it. Ed recognized the eye movement, looking slightly up and unfocused, small changes in facial expressions, trying not to give anything away.

Ed became angry. Part of the anger was a feeling of betrayal from the voice; he had carried it so long and served as its sole benefactor for so many years. Another part of the anger was from fear, knowing that he had lost his control over the thing, knowing that it could now grow without his influence. The final piece of his anger was his understanding that he would now have to step up and be brave when he didn't want to be.

I survived the First Russian Revolution, did what I had to do, came to this country with nothing. I worked and worked. I sold air conditioners for half a decade. I learned how people thought and became good at convincing them. I saved all my money, living in flophouses and then in my car for years. I never took anything for myself. I saved every penny, learned how the markets worked, invested, and made a fortune that I still don't spend. I sacrificed my life knowing the voice was out there, kept it busy waiting for years, kept it from hurting people.

Pastor Rick got a bizarre look on his face. He looked at Ed and turned his head sideways, a cross between shock, understanding, and confusion in his gaze.

"Ed. You are right; you were strong. You did all those things. I was proud of you for doing them," Pastor Rick said. It was his voice, but Ed picked up on the slightly different inflections to the language that the voice used.

Laundry must have recognized them too. He pushed his chair back and stood up, showing fear when he heard Pastor Rick speak.

Ed realized this meant that IX-Chel must have talked to both men at one time or another.

You can hear my thoughts?

"Yes," said IX-Chel using Pastor Rick as her medium.

Ed looked Rick in the eye. "Where are the children? Where are the two girls, Lara and Betty? Where are the two boys you just took, Billy and Ron?"

"Silly Edward!" It sounded even stranger coming from the body of Pastor Rick. "In some ways, you disappoint me, but in others, I remain gratified. You are who you are; your principles only bend so far! I find it ironic that now you worry about children when you saved me by sacrificing one to me when no one else would! Right at the end, at my last moment. It was the sweetest soul I ever ate!"

The thought never occurred to Ed what had happened to his sister's baby's soul when he saved the rest of his family from the soldiers.

Pastor Rick smiled a big smile. "Don't be shocked; what did you think had happened? At the time, I was gone, Edward. Depleted, spent. I was facing extinction, just like you were. Then this precious little offering comes out of nowhere. I needed strength, and there it was given to me freely. I was reborn! Eating it was euphoric! I still think about that moment. I loved you so much then!"

Ed felt sick. The old guilt was washing over him. "I never meant for it to happen that way. If I knew then what I know now, I never would have done it."

"The child would still have died, killed by the soldiers. Your mother and sister would have died. You would have died." Pastor Rick made a motion with his hand to emphasize this next point. "I would have died! You saved so many and gave up so little!"

"But their souls would have been safe from you!" Ed was overwhelmed but quickly regained himself, realizing that the voice never did anything by chance. It was trying to weaken him, distract him. He still had some level of control over it, or it at least it feared that he did.

What could it be? Damn.

"What could it be?" Pastor Rick mimicked. "I have told you a hundred times—I am an old god!" As he said it, he started to change, slowly growing in height as feathers sprang from his skin.

From outside, baleful wails flooded in, the tavern door still open, now filled with the sounds of children screaming in agony. Suddenly gunshots rang out, and within a few moments, Stone and Martha came sprinting in out of breath, Stone's pistol in his hand still smoking from being fired. Both Stone and Martha slid to a stop when they saw Pastor Rick. He was transforming into IX-

Chel right before their eyes

IX-Chel's transformation was slow and agonizing. The the monster started making its own horrible screeching noise, some combination of IX-Chel's glee and Pastor Rick's distress.

Ed started screaming at Stone. "Shoot it! Shoot it! Hurry before it is finished; it will be too strong!"

It took Stone just a moment to realize Ed was yelling at him and to regain himself from the sight of the transformation. He aimed his revolver and fired into the center of the beast. Three shots then reloaded and fired six more.

On impact, the sound was wet when it hit IX-Chel. The monster's noises evolved from evil glee to surprise and pain. Feathers, flesh, blood, and bone splattered out from the bullet wounds. The final shot was aimed at the center of the forming head, between the large owl eyes. On impact, it took the light out of them. IX-Chel fell, crumpled to the ground, still partially between IX-Chel's owl form and Pastor Rick's human frame.

The smoke from the pistol hung in the air. The room smelled like a combination of the gunshots, copper from all the blood, and a wet rotten swamp smell, presumably from IX-Chel. Everyone stood frozen, staring at the downed form. After a few moments, Stone moved, searching his belt for more ammunition.

"I'm out of bullets," he said matter-of-factly to

the room in general.

***

Laundry looked from IX-Chel's body to Stone, then to Ed, unsure which person to address. "Is it dead? Is that it? Can I get my children back now?"

The tortured noises from outside intensified. Three different voices were still crying out in agony from far off.

Stone started moving as he spoke. "Martha, close the door and start stacking tables and chairs in front of it." He turned to Ed, who was still dumbstruck. "Ed!"

Ed turned. "It's not dead."

"I know." Stone said firmly. "Where is Coral?"

"She ran out a few minutes ago. She is in on it, Judge. In on the land scam. I don't know about the rest. Maybe, I don't know."

"I need some help moving the tables," Martha said, having closed the door and put a few chairs in front of it.

Stone went over to help. "Ed, keep an eye on Laundry."

Ed nodded. He was already watching Laundry, not that he had any idea what to do if Laundry moved or tried anything.

Laundry was just standing, still in shock, looking down at Pastor Rick's body, such as it was.

It looked like Laundry's head was clearing some.

There was suddenly a deafening *bang* on the door. Both Martha and Stone, who were close to it, jumped back at the noise. It came again, the door vibrating and the tables and chairs shifting a little. A third bang followed; one of the chairs fell away. Martha stepped up and put it back.

"What are those things with the horns?" Laundry asked.

"My people call them the Windigo. They are spirit cannibals, eaters of men and boys. The larger they are, the more people they have eaten," Martha said.

"Jesus!" Laundry exclaimed.

"Not exactly," Stone returned, stepping into the middle of the room. "Mayor Laundry, we found your daughter, Lara."

Laundry allowed himself a look of optimism and hope, clearly not expecting Stone's statement. "Really? That's wonderful! Where is she?"

"You don't understand. We found her remains."

"No," Laundry said.

"I am afraid so," Stone said as there was another crash against the door. The hinges that held the door in place came partially undone.

"Martha," Stone said quickly, "do we have any options to dispel a Windigo?"

"Just what we already talked about. We have to eliminate her believers; they are giving her strength."

"There is only one left," Ed said. "The children are all dead. She has been using their life energy for the events we are witnessing. I think Laundry is her only remaining believer."

Just as Ed finished, Laundry began to make the same odd noise that Pastor Rick had made. He started the same process of transformation into IX-Chel. At the same moment, the door exploded inward, a huge Windigo bursting through, smashing the tables and chairs out of the way. There were two smaller Windigos following behind the big one.

Stone and Martha retreated to the center of the room, away from the horned monsters. Ed stepped towards them. Laundry's shrieks grew louder, and the gleeful mockery started again from IX-Chel as her form became dominant.

"Martha, Judge, get behind me," Ed said as he put himself in front of them, between them and the Windigos.

The monsters looked past Ed, but he moved left and right as they did, keeping himself in the way.

"Ed," Martha said, "do you know what you are doing?"

"No," he returned, some fear clearly in his voice.

"But I think I understand something now. I don't think they can hurt me. But be careful; they can kill either of you easily."

Stone watched. This was similar to what he had seen with spirits after they grew to understand themselves. He had never seen it happen with the living.

The large Windigo snarled at Ed, its lips pulled back and growling like a wolf. Ed advanced towards it, looking it in the mouth. The monster clearly was desperate to attack, but it didn't.

Ed walked very close to the monster, staring at it in the eyes now, showing no fear. He stopped when he was almost nose to nose and gathered himself. Then, all at once, he screamed at the top of his voice, as loud as he could, "Shut! Up! You!"

It seemed the sound waves leaving him were almost visible; they had that effect on the three monsters. As the words left his lips, they struck out at each beast, driving them back towards the door. Ed screamed again to the same result.

"Shut! Up! You!"

This second volley drove the Windigos back out the door, repelled again as the sound waves beat them like a force of nature. Like crashing waves on a beach or wind on a tree in a storm.

Quickly, Ed turned. "They will be stunned for a few minutes, not that long. Once IX-Chel is fully formed, they will return; she will command it. We only have maybe a minute or two." He looked around. "Judge, there is a hunting rifle behind the bar. Can you get it and shoot Laundry before the transformation is finished?"

Stone acted immediately, looking for the rifle and finding it after just a few moments' search. It was loaded and already primed. He checked for a safety; there wasn't one. There was a small magazine attached with a bolt-action loader. He hurriedly aimed and fired into Laundry. Again. Again. Seven times total, the final shot to the head just like Pastor Rick.

The results were the same; the body was killed mid-transformation.

As the report from the shots rang away, it was replaced with silence. The tortured screaming from outside had stopped. The scratching and noises from the Windigos had stopped. The inside of the tavern was silent except for Ed, Stone, and Martha's heavy breathing.

Both Pastor Rick and Mayor Laundry's bodies had slowly worked their way back to their natural human form, the exaggerated features and white feathers fading away. Both bodies were bloody, but it was a normal bloody mess, not a supernatural horror show.

Everyone stood for several minutes, slowly calming down.

Eventually, Ed said, "You said you found Lara, one of the girls. That she was dead. How did she die?"

Stone looked at him hard. "Badly," he said.

"Was it like the high schooler, Eric Adams?"

"More primitive, but yes, the same."

"When did it happen?" Ed had a look on his face that suggested he didn't want to know but that he needed to know.

"About a week ago, maybe a little longer. The body had been there. The elements and wildlife had been working on it."

"Judge, I heard screaming a week ago when I came out here for my retirement party. Coral told me it was rabbits. She was laughing!"

Stone just stared at Ed.

Martha made a face of disgust. "You think they all knew what was going on? That seems impossible."

"The screams were awful, and honestly, they sounded just like what we just heard out there. I assume those were the wails of Sally's boys?"

Stone shook his head with a realization. "We have to go find them now; maybe they are still alive." He started to move to the door.

"They are not, Judge. I can feel it," Ed said.

"Don't matter, Ed. We have to verify on the off

chance they are still alive out there. Even if the chance is minimal. If they are gone, we have to put them to rest; we can't leave children's bodies littered about the Everglades staked down and ripped open."

"Bahama Bill is still out there. He is a big fella who I think is dangerous," Ed returned.

"Maybe so." Stone looked at Martha and felt a responsibility to keep her safe, even if she would not have agreed with it. He knew a bit of how to get people to do what he needed.

"Martha, take Ed to Homestead. It's not safe around here; I can do all the cleanup work myself. Get the sheriff and bring him back. I don't know him, but when he gets here, I can explain things. Ed, Martha, just tell him what's here, not why. Tell him I am here, the Citrus County sheriff, and that I sent for him after I found the scene. Don't mention spirits or anything, just the bloody mess that we found."

"Absolutely not, Judge. I'm staying here," Martha said matter-of-factly.

"Please, just do it. I can handle things. This is what I do. It's easier if it's just me."

BAHAMA BILL

NOVEMBER 23, 3 A.M.

After a couple hours, Stone found the mutilated bodies and buried them in shallow graves, enough to put them to rest, not so deep it took a long time to dig them or that the county sheriff would have a hard time recovering them. They had been a mess, and the immediacy and freshness of the wounds made the going tough.

Moving the bodies and digging the graves got Stone even messier. To move the bodies, he had to pick them up, sometimes in pieces, getting child's blood and filth all over him. When digging the graves, the loose sand and dirt caked in the blood. It soaked his clothes all the way through. He repeated this many times, and by the time he was finished, he looked a horror show, completely drenched in gore from head to toe, much of it covered in blood-soaked dirt.

His eyes and teeth were a bright white shining

through the gunk. He had taken the hunting rifle after reloading it with cartridges he found under the bar, and he carried it with him now. It held nine rounds, plus one in the chamber. The rifle was old but had been well cared for, oiled, and adequately stowed. The moon wasn't out; the night was very dark. He had been out and away from other lights now long enough to have decent night vision, but anything farther than a few yards was still near impossible to see.

The easiest way to find Bill and Sally is going to be to retrace their steps. If I start back near the town, there should be tracks just a little farther out than all the commotion from earlier.

He turned and headed back, not that far away.

What do I do with Bill when I find him? What about the baker lady, Sally? Her children were just brutally murdered. Does she know? Things could get messy quick.

Stone searched for about twenty minutes, eventually finding what looked like the tracks of two people, one heavier than the other by a good deal. The tracks headed west down the white dirt and sand road on the other side of the small town, away from civilization and further into the Everglades. He followed it, deciding to go for about thirty minutes before turning back. He didn't have to go that long; a few minutes down the road was a Florida Cracker ranch.

Even Stone had been confused with the name Cracker when he migrated to Florida from Colorado ten years ago. The term apparently evolved from a whip's sound when it snaps, sounding like a firecracker. The men wielding the whip, therefore, were called crackers.

In Colorado, Stone had done some livestock farming. His friend Jack Abbott had owned Abbott Farms, breeding horses, some of the finest for the time. In Colorado, they didn't use whips. Not out of concern for the animals, but because they didn't have to. Horse-mounted cowboys and good dogs could herd the animals where needed; there was plenty of flat open ground to maneuver. In Florida, so much of the land was covered in palmetto bushes and other weeds and shrubbery that livestock often wandered down trails and into confined areas, making the whip, as motivation to move the animal, a necessity to a successful drive and herd management.

Anyway, the name has stuck and was becoming slang for poor whites in Florida in general.

The ranch was relatively new, built in a slightly modified structure from the ones Stone new from Colorado, less of an angle to the roof. There was no need to worry about snow accumulation. This ranch had firelight coming from the inside. The main house was a relatively small structure, probably a main living area, bedroom, and maybe a storage pantry. As Stone approached, he could see a shadow moving through the small high windows.

Okay, announce myself or peak in the window and risk getting shot as an intruder? Well, I guess I am an intruder, so window it is.

He moved to the side, off the main path to the house door. When he got close, he carefully looked in the window, most of his body off to the side.

Well, of course, what else was I expecting? This is a terrible night.

It wasn't that he had hardened in the last several hours to bloodshed and carnage. He had hardened to it years ago, during the Civil War, and in the decades after. He had now seen half a dozen mutilated bodies in just the past couple of hours. He had shot and killed two men as they transformed into a giant white bird-thing. But *still,* this scene was unnecessarily gruesome and brutal; hard to understand.

Bill, Bahama Bill, sat on the wood and dirt floor of the house in the dim orange firelight. Sally's body was next to him, her head missing, most of the blood from her body emptied out onto the floor from the now-open neck. Bill had used his hands to rip open her chest and abdomen. He sat eating what was probably her stomach and lungs. So much had been pulled out and moved around, there was still so much blood, it was a little hard to be sure.

Martha had said the horned things were called Wendigo and that they were cannibals. The larger the Wendigo, the more men it had eaten. Bill must have been the giant one that came through the door; he was a big man. Now back here, trying to gain power by eating Sally.

It didn't seem to be working, though. He was eating frantically to no effect.

Suddenly he stopped and looked up to the closed door, smelling the air, turning his head to focus on what he heard.

He smells the blood of the children on me. There is still some Wendigo in him, even though he has mostly changed back.

Stone himself was a big man with broad shoulders and a sturdy build. Not as large as Bahama Bill, but big enough to hold his own and strong enough to end any fight. He also had an extra fifty years of being in a thirty-five-year-old body, enough time to master numerous fighting styles, both fair and dirty.

It did not look like Bill saw Stone in the window, so Stone carefully but quickly moved away, going a few dozen yards back the way he came, keeping his eyes on the door. He got as far as he could to still be able to see the door clearly. He knelt down, checked the rifle load, and waited.

It didn't take long. The door opened, and Bill emerged, fearless and on the hunt, stopping in the doorframe and smelling the air again. He was naked and covered in blood, still walking partially hunched over. The Windigos ran on all fours.

Stone aimed the rifle but didn't fire. He wanted to see what Bill was going to do.

Suddenly Bill lifted his head and screeched into the air. It was a bloodcurdling noise, a combination of a canine howl, a human cry, and some otherworldly echo. It was loud and sent a chill down Stone's back.

In the distance, two calls came in return.

That would be the other two monsters. But who are they? I found all the children's bodies already.

Bill snapped his head around as though he heard Stone's thought, looking right at him. Stone fired and missed. He expertly cycled the bolt and fired again and missed again. The first shot had missed the house completely; the second impacted the wall about four feet to Bill's left.

This thing has a hell of a pull.

Stone adjusted for the sights, aiming four feet to Bill's right. But Bill broke into a run, heading right at him, covering the ground quickly. Stone pulled the trigger, cycled the bolt, pulled the trigger, cycled the bolt, repeating over and over until the ammo was gone.

Several shots landed, slowing Bill. They were not precise shots, impacting all over Bill's body, and none provided a kill shot. Stone dropped the rifle just as Bill landed on him. The impact from the momentum was hard and caused both men to lose their balance and roll. Instead of swinging his arms, Bill was trying to get hold of Stone and bite him. Stone noticed Bill's slightly elongated jaw, not yet fully restored to his human form from his earlier transformation.

Bill was also *strong,* stronger than the big man should have been. He was overpowering Stone, able to get his mouth close to Stone's right shoulder. Stone's left hand was free; he used all the force and strength he had with his right arm to keep Bill away, but he was losing the battle. He frantically searched the ground, sight unseen, able to dislodge a fist-sized rock partially buried in the soft sandy dirt.

Bill was close, able to sink his teeth into Stone's shoulder. Any closer to Stone's neck and the bite would be fatal. The pain was near debilitating. Stone screamed, freed the rock, and began bashing it into the right side of Bill's head with his left hand, using all of his might, over and over, screaming in pain and rage at the same time.

Eventually, the bite pressure subsided. Stone continued beating the rock into Bill's head, now just a wet mass of brain and smashed skull bones. Two other smaller monsters were running at him; he saw them, resigned to the fact that there was no way to fight them. He was too injured and near defenseless. However, they faded from sight in a dead run as Bill's life finally flowed away.

Bill was the last true believer. With him gone, the monsters are gone, and anything they controlled is now free, was Stone's final thought as he lost consciousness.

MIAMI HOSPITAL

NOVEMBER 25, 1919, 10 A.M. (THANKSGIVING)

The hospital had several open floors with hundreds of empty beds, still in its configuration to deal with large amounts of sick as the Spanish Flu pandemic faded from its 1918 frantic height. Big slow-moving fans tried to move the air in the room, succeeding somewhat with the reduced late November temperatures and fewer patients. There were beds in rows of a hundred, six columns deep. Each bed was made with a clean-looking white sheet and a modest pillow. Each bed frame was identical, painted a middle-tone gray with a single mattress on a spring.

Stone had grabbed an unused pillow from the empty bed next to him so he could comfortably sit up. He had a pile of newspapers from the past week next to his bed; he was reading them in order so he could get caught back up to the goings-on and bring himself current. He was using a doctor's chair as a table and had a cup of coffee on it, still steaming. The big news in the papers was a dance-hall fire in Louisiana that left fifty people dead.

I'll need to keep an eye on Louisiana; there may be more going on there than meets the eye.

Stone had learned over the years to monitor the papers; it was what initially brought him to Citrus County, Florida. Ten years prior, the *Citrus County Chronicle* reported a story that was picked up nationally about a new lighthouse that seemed to be leading ships to ruin instead of safety. That case ended up being a harrowing supernatural experience with the shadows in full force, so much so Stone decided to stick around for a decade to deal with all the fallout.

He turned the page of the *Miami Herald* with his left hand, the right shoulder wrapped in bandages, then took another sip of his coffee.

"Judge, you're awake!" Martha yelled as she hurried over. She was wearing dirty work clothes with automotive grease on them, a white men's undershirt, and blue-jean overalls. Her hair was pulled back and tied into a bun. Ed walked behind her, a good foot shorter, wearing the same thing. The two looked to be in makeshift uniforms of sorts.

Martha ran and embraced Stone; the two kissed

familiarly. Ed stood back just a little to let the moment happen, waving his hand at Stone when the hug was finished, and Stone looked up.

"Oh, I'm sorry, Judge," Martha said, a big smile on her face. "I got grease on your clean white blankets!"

"That's okay, I can just change beds; there are plenty to choose from." He smiled back, happy to see Martha and surprised at himself for being glad to see Ed Leeds as well. "What on earth are you two tinkering with? You look like you just repaired an army tank!" Tanks were brand new, having just been used in the Great War in Europe eighteen months before; they were very much in the public consciousness.

Martha's smile stayed big. "Almost! I have been helping Ed convert his Model 31 into a pick-up truck with a winch and pulley system!"

Ed nodded. "Martha has been a great help. We got the conversion finished about twice as fast as if I did it by myself."

Stone folded his newspaper and drank more of his coffee. "That's an expensive car to be pulling apart."

Ed nodded his agreement. "It's true, but it all worked out well. The side of the car was ruined, with deep scratch marks. But the Model 31 is a beast." Ed immediately regretted his words. "Er, has a big frame. I'm happy with it."

The joviality left the conversation at the mention of beast.

"Well, speaking of beasts," Stone said, "how is Florida City? I talked to the Dade County people yesterday, but they didn't tell me anything other than we are all in the clear."

"The buildings are still there, but the little town is all but finished," Martha said. "They found that everyone living within about three miles had been killed. There is no one left."

Ed made a grim face. "It was bad, Judge. IX-Chel promises to bring life but instead consumes it all. I have a feeling it's what these old gods do. The more powerful they became, the more life they consumed to maintain their power. I am so lucky that you helped. I didn't know what to do, but I could see how I would have been outmatched. Thank goodness we were able to stop IX-Chel before she had dozens or hundreds of believers. She was so powerful with just the six or seven and a few residences to sacrifice."

Everyone nodded their agreement; it had been a close call.

"So, Ed, what's your plan? What are you going to do now?" Stone asked.

"I'm going to do what I always planned on doing. The plot of land I bought is extraordinary. It is positioned such that magnetic forces have amplified powers. Since I first heard the voice, I have been studying. Studying ancient manuscripts from Egypt and the pyramids. Working to understand what the voice was and how to kill it.

"I know it's gone now, no more believers. But I will still construct a machine that can capture and banish these—what do you call them, shadows? These shadows. This way, if a new one ever shows up, and I suspect one will eventually, we'll have the tools necessary to deal with it without all the bloodshed and risk and dangers of what we just went through."

Stone didn't think that made any sense. He knew the truth of the shadows, but he couldn't find a reason to try and talk Ed out of something he had been planning for half his life. "What will this machine be? How will it work?"

Ed smiled. "I can't give all my secrets away! Do you know about the Egyptian pyramids?"

"No," Stone said. "Are they like the one in Crystal River? I know something about that one."

"Not really. The one here was very small. There are much larger versions in Mexico, but they are not like the ones in Egypt. The ones here are what are called step pyramids. While very advanced, in the end, they are just rocks piled higher and higher on terraces. Each new level a little smaller in, like a flight of stairs. In Mexico, most of the old ones have a structure on the top."

Stone nodded that he understood.

Ed continued. "But Judge, Martha...in Egypt, the pyramids are huge, hundreds of feet tall. They have some that are as tall as the Eiffel Tower! Made from millions of giant stone blocks. Each block by itself can be dozens or even hundreds of tons."

"Wow," Stone said, impressed at both the description and Ed's enthusiasm for the topic.

"So I have been reading about them. The Egyptians have hundreds of ancient texts that explain how the structures were built. I'm going to follow the same procedure here in Florida and build a giant structure. See, once it's built, gravity and even time work differently. By adding in an electrical current, I know I can capture spirits like IX-Chel."

"How could you know that? Why would you even think it?" Stone asked, curious.

"Because of the old books from what they call the Old Kingdom. From five thousand years ago, that talk about spirits, what you call shadows. They describe a war between this world and the shadow world. The Egyptians built all these huge pyramids as a way to win the war. If the shadows are coming back, and let's be honest, Judge, we know they are; we just fought one. But if they are coming back, someone needs to be ready for them."

Stone nodded, not really convinced or even

understanding but not wanting to be negative; the idea was undoubtedly in the right direction. "Sounds good to me, Ed. You've got Martha and my support for sure." Then a thought hit him. "Where have you been staying? Not in the abandoned town?"

Martha laughed, "Oh no way! That place is a crime scene. Do you remember Pastor Carry? She was the colored pastor."

"Yes, I remember her. Nice lady."

"She is letting us stay at the parish next to her church. It is about halfway between Ed's property and Florida City."

"That's fantastic," Stone said, meaning it. "The doctor wants to keep me here one more day even though I feel fine. I have been on the phone with Jorge, and the air flights are running tomorrow just like every Friday, even with the holiday. Martha, do you think you can pull yourself away from your new mechanic's career to fly back with me?"

She laughed. "Of course! Ed, that means you can drive me around in your truck today and show me how the pulley system works!"

Ed smiled, feeling about as happy as he ever had. A pretty girl he could show off to for the next day and a lot of exciting work to start to do.

This is going to be a new beginning! someone

thought with great eagerness and delight.

HOUND & PUB

JULY 1920, SEVERAL MONTHS LATER

Prohibition started in January 1920. No more bars, pubs, or alcohol. The Hound & Pub, Stone's home away from home, closed. The owner abandoned the structure, rumored to have moved off to New York City to open a deli. Stone negotiated with the city office and was able to get the deed to the building for just the cost of the back taxes.

He quit—well, "retired"—from the Citrus County sheriff position. His recommendation to the county commissioners as the new sheriff was Jorge, but no one seemed much interested in an Indian Sheriff, so Bonaparte "Bone" Mizell, the deputy with the second most seniority, was appointed as temporary sheriff until the elections in November.

Stone and Martha decided to live together but not seek legal marriage. They could have been legally married in Florida as it did not have anti-miscegenation laws like several states did. Instead, though, they decided to follow the native Indian custom, simply announcing that they were a couple without any ceremony or formal gathering.

They both worked hard for the first part of the year, converting the front of the pub into a small café and the back into an apartment they lived in. Martha could cook, and as Stone put it, he could stand in the front and take people's money with little effort. From the start, they had county deputies in every day for two, sometimes three meals. It quickly got the reputation of having good food at a fair price and being the safest place in Citrus County, between Stone's steely gazes and the constant patronage of law officers.

They knocked out the front of the old bar and put in big windows, bringing in natural light. There were eight tables and a short counter-bar with ten seats. Ed got Stone in contact with an air conditioning distributor in Tampa. Stone got a very good deal on air conditioning for the café and the apartment in the back. It changed everything; Ed had been correct; the units paid for themselves with additional patrons in just a couple months.

So much so the place had a waiting line for breakfast and lunch. No one much came for dinner, so Stone started closing at 3 p.m. It made for a good life with plenty of personal time, and the money was more than adequate even with the low prices, mainly because of the high volume of customers. They made so much money they bought a used car and opened a bank savings account in both their names. Martha had taken Stone's name, which made the whole process easier.

Things went well, and Stone and Martha enjoyed each other's company a great deal. So much so that often, flashes of light could be seen under their closed bedroom door most nights.

Stone negotiated to be a distributor for the *Miami Herald* and the *Tampa Tribune.* A bundle of twenty papers for each was dropped off every day between breakfast and lunch. Stone spent every afternoon reading both papers and just enjoying his time talking to people who came to the café and living in the apartment with Martha.

On Thursday, July 1st, 1920, a man in a dark suit came to the café between the breakfast and lunch crowds. He was a greasy man; his suit looked overused and under-washed.

"I am looking for Issac Stone," he said.

"That's me." Stone stood up from his usual spot behind the counter, near the cash register, putting down his newspaper from yesterday.

The man nodded, largely disinterested. "Mr. Stone. I represent the Miami City law firm Sterwits

& Goldman, Esquire. We are the executors of a will that is currently in probate. A Mr. Edward Leedskalnin, of Florida City, Florida."

"I see," Stone said, realizing this meant that Ed had passed.

"You and a woman named Martha Washington..." The man looked up from his paper. "Is that really her name?"

Irritation flashed through Stone, but he didn't let it show. "She is Martha Stone now."

The man smirked as though he had discovered some irony. "Of course. The two of you are named as beneficiaries in the will."

"How did Ed die?" Stone asked, working through his emotions.

The man made a face of irritation at being interrupted. "I don't know that, sir. May I finish?"

Stone nodded. "Of course."

Martha heard the conversation from the back through the short-order window and came around to listen, wiping her hands on her cook apron.

"Are you Martha?" the greasy man in the dark suit asked as he watched her approach.

"Yes."

"Both of you are requested to come to our Tampa office at your earliest convenience, but no later than July tenth of this year, for the reading of the will."

Stone stood up and put his arm around Martha; she was starting to process the information and was becoming sad, realizing this meant that Ed had passed.

"We can close for lunch and go now, Judge," Martha said, starting to untie her apron and take it off.

The man did not miss a beat. "I will notify my office that you will be there today at 4 p.m. Is that satisfactory?"

"That's fine," Stone said.

***

Stone and Martha arrived about thirty minutes early, pulling their Ford Model-T into the parking lot outside the law building. It was on the opposite side of the street from the courthouse in downtown Tampa, the corner of Jackson Street and Jefferson Street. They both wore their dark sunglasses, secretly liking how it made them look together, mysterious and strong. Not knowing what else to wear, they put on their dark clothes, the same ones they had worn to Eric Adams's funeral back in November.

Stone applied the brake and turned off the car, getting out and holding the door for Martha as she exited. They walked into the building and, after a few minutes of conversation, were directed into a large conference room where they waited. The room demonstrated immense wealth, mahogany bookshelves, polished tables, leather chairs, gold lamps. The floor was covered with an oriental rug over gleaming hardwood.

Martha sat quiet, feeling small. She had been crying, thinking about Ed and how happy he was the last time she saw him, how far he had come, and how brave he was when he needed to be, fighting the shadow monster. Stone paced up and down the long wall, looking out the window from time to time, waiting, not at all certain what to expect.

After nearly an hour, the door finally opened. Two men and a woman entered. One man was older with white hair wearing a very distinguished business suit. The other was younger, carrying a stack of papers. The woman wore working office clothes and had a paper pad, some loose papers in a notebook, and three pens.

The older man stepped forward confidently and extended his hand to Stone. "Mr. Stone, sir. I am Harold Sterwits, and this is my firm." They shook hands; it was an overly firm shake. "My apologies for the wait. I wanted to be here for this, not relegate you to a partner." He looked at Martha, then said, "Has no one offered you something to drink?" There was an edge to his voice that suggested a tremendous faux pas had been committed.

"That's fine, sir," Stone said. "We are a little in the dark here and would like to get things moving."

"Yes, of course, Mr. Stone. My apologies nonetheless. Please, sit down. You too, young miss. You both are included in this equally." He took a seat on one side of the big, long, polished table, indicating two chairs on the other side for Stone and Martha.

As everyone settled, Sterwits nodded to the man, who handed him an envelope from his pile of papers.

"My instructions—" Sterwits looked at Stone, then Martha. "I'm sorry, is it Mr. and Mrs.?"

Martha nodded.

"Mr. and Mrs. Stone, my instructions are to read you this letter as written by Mr. Leedskalnin. I am to read it to you as written in its entirety. Then I can explain the rest of the information. Is that acceptable?"

Both Stone and Martha nodded.

Sterwits put on a pair of reading glasses and unfolded the letter. He looked at it, looked over his glasses at Stone and Martha, then back to the letter.

> *Dear Martha and Judge:*
>
> *I hired this shill-lawyer company to handle my estate. They are pirates and*

> *expensive as hell, but they are pre-paid, so don't let them slack off on their duties which they will try and do.*

Sterwits paused, looked back at Stone and Martha, smiled, cleared his throat, and continued.

> *But they seem capable enough. I won't go into too many details since the pirate lawyers are sitting right here, but you remember them anyway. I got much of my castle built, but it didn't work. We all made one mistake. We forgot that I believed too. Bahama Bill wasn't the last one; I was.*
>
> *I realized this and hoped the machine would do its job, but it didn't. Nevertheless, I have learned that our initial approach was correct; there wasn't any other way. All believers had to be dealt with. You can surmise how things went since you are in a lawyer's office getting this read to you. I had to do it myself. It was a lot harder than I thought it would be.*
>
> *Anyway, no complaints.*
>
> *I wanted you both to know that between the two of you, you were the nicest to me that anyone ever was in my whole life. And, you are the only people to ever buy me anything.*

DAVID EDWARD

You bought me breakfast at the Rascal House Diner.

You also left a ridiculous tip, so I hope you manage my money better than you manage your own.

Between that breakfast and Martha, you helping me work on my car without asking for any payment and being all pretty and pleasant when you did it, well, I think you understand. You are good people, and I wish you the best.

I am leaving my estate to you. I came to America with nothing and worked my whole life. You are about to find out how well I did, and I can tell you that this is a meager gift that does not compare to what your kindness meant to me, even with all the other goings-on.

The fat-cat city lawyers here are going to kiss your butt now. That's okay, let them. They are getting a hefty sum that they won't earn. I am also leaving my Florida City property to you. I would like for you to hire a caretaker and open it to the world for tours. It is a modern marvel. Remind people what one small immigrant can do in the world's greatest country.

Oh, but make sure you charge

something. Ten cents should be enough, but something. I'm sure I would turn over in my grave if I found out people were tromping all over the place for free.

Ed.

Martha could not hold her tears back anymore and was crying.

Stone looked confused. "When did Ed die?"

"A week ago," Sterwits said. "You two really have no idea, do you?"

It was hard to read his comment. A wave of irritation caught Stone. "Why don't you enlighten us before I lose my temper?" he said with a wave of anger at the drawn-out explanation.

Sterwits made a face of surprise. "Sorry, we usually deal with squabbling relatives fighting each other. Anyway"—he nodded to the man with the pile of papers again and got handed another single sheet—"Mr. Leedskalnin has left you his entire estate, after probate and legal fees. Its current value is seven million four hundred thousand dollars. However, a good portion of that is in Coca-Cola stock, which is in high demand due to prohibition, so the exact value is accurate as of yesterday; the stock continues to appreciate. His estate also includes the property mentioned earlier in Florida City and an eight thousand dollar modified Model 31 sedan."

"How did he die?" Stone asked. He was trying to understand what had happened. He didn't register the amount of money involved on first hearing.

The woman with the notepad and pens started to arrange the table and lay out papers. Sterwits looked at Stone for a moment; the two men were in different headspaces.

"It was an accident on site; he was crushed under a giant coral slab that slipped off scaffolding he had built to hold it in place," Sterwits said.

"Was there a funeral?" Martha asked. "We would have liked to have attended."

Stone shook his head. "I read the papers every day, including the Miami paper. I didn't see any mention of this or an obituary."

"Ed specifically asked that we not publish an obituary." Sterwits flipped through some papers on the table, realizing something. "How do you want to receive the funds?"

"What funds?" Stone said, appreciating that he might need to focus on what the lawyer was telling him.

"The money and stock from the estate," Sterwits said.

Stone shook his head. "Mr. Sterwits, I'm sorry to seem unenlightened, but I don't understand what you are asking. Receive what?"

"Do you have a bank, Mr. Stone?"

"Yes, Martha and I have a joint account at the Suncoast Credit Union. We needed it for the café revenues."

Sterwits nodded and thought. "That's a small bank, Mr. Stone. Might I recommend you open an account at the First National Bank? They are much better equipped to handle an account in the, well, range, of your account."

The light clicked for Stone. "How much money did you say?"

"Seven million four hundred thousand dollars. Roughly a third of that is cash, and the other two-thirds are in a stock portfolio."

The numbers started to sink in this time.

"What is a stock portfolio?" Martha asked.

Sterwits leaned back in his chair, understanding now what he was dealing with.

"Mr. and Mrs. Stone," he said calmly, "I think you are going to be very happy when I tell you."

EDWARD LEEDSKALNIN

ABOUT A WEEK EARLIER

Ed, I don't think the machine thingy you built is working the way you hoped.

The day was hot. Ed was sweating. The damn voice was back. It was small and nice like a long time ago.

"It should have worked," he returned.

We have a lot of fo work to do, Ed, you and me. We have to start over. It took me six months to come back, clinging to the smallest part of your light, that little tiny spark of you that can never forget me.

Ed sat down on the dais in the middle of the grand coral structure he had built all by himself. It looked like a castle—large coral building blocks, twenty-foot-high walls, towers, and many different structures, each with a very specific purpose.

Do you want to recheck it? I would hate to deprive

you of this last chance of getting rid of me. I do have to tell you, I find this upsetting. I love you now, of course. But I might have a hard time getting past you trying to capture my spirit and banish it, you know, if things pick up again.

"Do you feel any gravity at all? Any force pulling you?"

Nope! Now remember, Ed, I have explained this several times. There are three parts to a soul: intellect, energy, and appetite. Which part are the magnets supposed to affect?

Ed had been through this is his studying, the ancient texts being unambiguous. "The magnets should trap your energy between them. They represent positive and negative energy flow."

You should have just asked me before this elaborate scheme! You misunderstood the instructions. Oh, Ed. This is so tragic for you. You messed up, and now I know everything. You should have had that Indian woman help and the big scary man she goes with. They would have figured it out, just like they did the first time.

"Voice, we know each other too well now. You want me to bring them back because together, their light is so bright you could have used it as a beacon to return sooner. Separately they each have sway, but together they are something new and different."

Silly! Well, I guess we do know each other at this

point. So for your machine, here is where you went wrong. You forgot what I told you about the three parts. I told you so many times. You didn't align them correctly. You can't try energy between positive and negative; that's not how it works. You have to align things.

So you are right that I am energy, but I am also intellect and appetite. Intellect is the positive, and appetite the negative. That's the complete puzzle. You built this whole thing for just a fraction of it.

It all made sense now; he could see how it all fit together. The voice was right, though. It would take a year to reconfigure the structure to account for all three elements. He had made a mistake. He ran some numbers in his head, to work right, the property was too far south; he needed to move everything about ten miles north and east, closer to Homestead.

"I'll never be able to rebuild it in time, will I?"

Not now that I know, Ed.

"Is there anything I can do?"

No, and Ed, I do love you, but I have to let you know that it's not going to go easy like last time. You have done some things that are going to be hard for me to get past. I'm afraid we are in for some extremely long, painful nights together.

Ed sighed. He knew what was required, resigning himself to it over the past couple of weeks. He reached over and pulled the rope attached to the scaffolding, not wanting to, but having learned how to be brave when it counted.

The End.